JEWISH MOTHERS
NEVER DIE

JEWISH MOTHERS
NEVER DIE

A NOVEL

NATALIE
DAVID-WEILL

TRANSLATED BY MOLLY GROGAN

ARCADE PUBLISHING
NEW YORK

Arcade Publishing books may be purchased in bulk at special discounts for sales promotion, corporate gifts, fund-raising, or educational purposes. Special editions can also be created to specifications. For details, contact the Special Sales Department, Arcade Publishing, 307 West 36th Street, 11th Floor, New York, NY 10018 or arcade@skyhorsepublishing.com.

Arcade Publishing® is a registered trademark of Skyhorse Publishing, Inc.®, a Delaware corporation.

Visit our website at www.arcadepub.com.

10 9 8 7 6 5 4 3 2

Library of Congress Cataloging-in-Publication Data is available on file.

ISBN: 978-1-62872-791-3
Ebook ISBN: 978-1-62872-794-4

Printed in the United States of America

Three mothers are bragging about how much their sons spoil them.

The first one says: "My son loves me so much that for my last birthday, he gave me a fur coat."

Not to be outdone, the second one crows: "Is that all? My son saved up for a year to send me on a cruise in the Caribbean."

As for the third, she has them both beat. "My son is the most extraordinary of all," she gloats. "He sees a shrink three times a week just so he can talk about me."

For Charles, Paul, and Marie

THE MOTHERS
(in chronological order)

- Amalia Freud, née Nathanshon (1835–1930). Wife of Jacob. Mother of Sigmund, Julius, Anna, Rosa, Mitzi, Dolfi, Paula and Alexander
- Jeanne Proust, née Weil (1849–1905). Wife of Adrien. Mother of Marcel and Robert
- Pauline Einstein, née Koch (1858–1920). Wife of Hermann. Mother of Albert and Maja
- Minnie Marx, née Schönberg (1865–1929). Wife of Samuel. Mother of the Marx Brothers: Leonard (Chico), Adolph (Harpo), Julius (Groucho), Milton (Gummo), and Herbert (Zeppo)
- Louise Cohen, née Ferro (1870–1945). Wife of Marco. Mother of Albert
- Mina Kacew, née Iosselevna-Borisovskaia (1883–1941). Wife of Ariah. Mother of Romain (known as Romain Gary)
- Nettie Königsberg, née Cherry (1906–2002). Wife of Martin. Mother of Allan (known as Woody Allen) and Letty

1

A Mother's Heaven

*God couldn't be everywhere, so he
created mothers.*

Jewish proverb

"She's crying. I think she's crying."

"How come? "

"Maybe she doesn't realize she's dead?"

"That's no reason to be sad."

"You've obviously forgotten the state you were in when you showed up in Jewish Mothers' Heaven."

"How would you know? You weren't even here yet yourself."

"I heard all about it."

"Whatever you say, Miss Know it all."

Still bickering, the two elderly ladies shuffled closer to Rebecca, who lay, silent tears streaming down her cheeks. How could she be crying? She never lamented. She'd forgotten what it was like to cry, or to be confused, or even surprised. But the tears still came, as if her whole body was slipping out of her grasp, as if she was no longer even trying to hold on. She couldn't understand what was happening to her. Until that very moment, she had always succeeded in avoiding the unexpected. Long ago, she had decided to take control of her life, her destiny and her emotions. She had imposed the most rigorous self-discipline and had followed it to the letter. She loved order the way other people enjoyed a relaxing vacation. She had lists for everything: errands, books she had read and books she meant to

2 • JEWISH MOTHERS NEVER DIE

read (the longest list by far), ideas, trips, appointments . . . Rebecca left nothing to chance.

To be caught so completely off guard was bewildering. What had happened and where was she? She looked more closely at the two women: they were old enough to be her grandmothers, or more likely her great-grandmothers, judging from their Twenties-era gowns. Had she gone back in time? Was this a costume party? Why were they staring and whispering? Was this someone's home, one of theirs? She tried to get to her feet, using a table for support. Why did she notice the quality of the mahogany when she felt so utterly forlorn?

The smaller of the two women motioned to Rebecca to sit down on an overstuffed black velour sofa. Her almond-shaped, dark eyes were vividly made-up, but their beauty couldn't hide her time-worn features or the fact that her lace dress and hat, whose netting was turned up at one corner, looked straight from a vintage rag shop. Yet her plumpness gave her an air of confidence. She smiled benevolently at Rebecca and asked in a kind voice:

"What's your name, dear?"

"Rebecca Rosenthal. What's yours?"

"I'm Louise Cohen, Albert's mother," the little woman replied. "I imagine you've heard of him..."

"Albert Cohen's mother? The author of *Belle du Seigneur* is your son?" Rebecca couldn't hide the awe she always felt at meeting someone famous.

"Didn't I tell you that Albert was famous?" Louise gushed, turning towards her taller, more imposing companion, who shot back competitively:

"And the Marx Brothers? I suppose you've heard of them?"

"Don't tell me you're their mother, too?"

Minnie Marx burst out laughing, giving Rebecca the opportunity to study her more closely: finger waves crowned her round, over-powdered face, marking a stark contrast with her brightly painted lips and black dress, which was held in place at the breast by a brooch. She came straight from an Erckmann-Chatrian novel, Rebecca thought.

"They never would have become famous without me!"

"That's quite enough bragging, Minnie; you'll tire Rebecca."

"On the contrary," interjected Rebecca. "I adore the Marx Brothers. When I was younger, I went every Sunday to see their films. My favorites were *Duck Soup* and *Room Service*. They were the best medicine for a dull childhood! I loved Groucho's big black mustache—that New York accent, that sense of the absurd. He always made me laugh the most."

"More than Chico?" Minnie wondered.

Not wanting to disappoint the mother of the Marx Brothers, Rebecca launched into her memories.

"They were all so funny. What I liked best, though, was finding the same scenes in all the films: Harpo at his harp, Chico's Italian accent, and Margaret Dumont, always so indignant when she found she'd been tricked all over again by that irresistible Groucho."

"I can see you're pretty taken with Groucho," remarked Minnie.

"Whoever thought up the 'walk this way' gag was a genius," Rebecca added.

Minnie couldn't stop herself from laughing heartily again while imitating Groucho's characteristic stooped gait and cigar-smoking.

"How is it you have nothing to say about Albert?" wondered Louise Cohen out loud.

"I was enthralled by *Belle du Seigneur!* Solal is intelligent, handsome, seductive and so wretched, I was crazy about him. I always thought the author must have been very much like him."

Louise Cohen blushed with pride.

"Exactly! Even if he always denied it, Albert was like Solal, his hero, in more ways than one."

It seemed to Rebecca as if she were taking a test for which no one had told her the question. All she could be sure of was that she was expected to display an encyclopedic knowledge of the Marx Brothers and Albert Cohen and shower them with praises. She'd managed well enough so far but she was surprised by how much she wanted to pass this exam when its purpose remained unclear. What was the point of placating these women? Was she really dead? How could she have died and not know it? She hadn't traveled through any tunnel, hadn't seen any white light. Her life hadn't flashed before her eyes . . .

"I heard you say I was dead. That's impossible. I didn't feel anything."

"You just don't remember," Minnie said gently.

Louise Cohen asked her what had happened just before she arrived there.

"Nothing."

Rebecca looked herself over. She recognized her favorite green sweater, her suede pants that showed off her legs so well, her high-heeled boots that pinched her feet. The only unfamiliar thing was her surroundings: she was in a sort of living room she had never seen before.

"What is the last thing you remember?" Louise Cohen asked again.

"Stop torturing the poor girl!" protested Minnie. "She's had quite a shock already. Leave her alone!"

"You're the one who started it, Minnie. Don't blame me. Rebecca is fine, just a bit confused. There's nothing unusual about that."

How could these women talk about her as if she wasn't there? Rebecca, who hated any violation of her privacy, felt like the new girl at boarding school who hadn't yet gotten her bearings. The whole thing was impossible. Could she really be sitting with the mothers of Albert Cohen and the Marx Brothers? How did they know each other? And why did they continue to sit together if they only argued about everything?

"You were asking me if I could remember anything," Rebecca ventured. Curiosity was getting the best of her. What did she have to lose?

"I remember being thrown from my car. I remember that the rain was soaking my clothes and, a few seconds later, I felt a terrible pain."

Minnie took pity on her:

"How old are you? You're just a child."

"Thirty-eight. That's not all that young, you know."

"That depends on the person."

Louise Cohen took Minnie Marx by the arm and whispered that this was no time to ruin everything. For once something new was happening, she wanted all the details. Angering Rebecca wouldn't help her admit that she was dead. If they went about this the wrong way, it could upset her even more and she might refuse to tell them anything, or worse, go away!

Minnie dismissed her companion's argument with a wave of the hand:

"It's not Rebecca you're trying to spare but yourself."

"Do you have anything better to do?" despaired Louise.

"No, you're right."

Together they turned to face Rebecca once again. She was deep in thought.

"So, it was a car accident?" said ventured Louise, hoping to start Rebecca talking.

Rebecca began to tremble, and the pain that had crushed her earlier struck her again with sudden force.

"We're here to help you," offered Minnie in a disarmingly gentle tone of voice. "We know exactly what you're feeing."

The two women watched her patiently. They waited. They had nothing but time. Rebecca tried to remember more. Speaking softly, she recounted the facts as they had happened.

"I couldn't see anything and the minutes dragged on. I had hair and mud in my eyes but I could make out other cars. Strangely, they appeared to be driving sideways. I thought it would make a beautiful scene in a film, as if it was all taking place far from me. In fact, I was lying on the asphalt and I could see the traffic on the highway from underneath my car. Anyone else would have tried to hold on, but not me; I wanted it to end as quickly as possible. I could hear footsteps, people running and calling in my direction, sirens in the distance... That's when I lost consciousness, I think."

She was panic-stricken now at the thought of her own premature death and everything she had left undone. So many appointments that week alone. She was far too busy to die!

"Busy with what?" Minnie wanted to know.

"I'm a French professor at the Sorbonne. I have lectures to prepare, exams to correct, students to check up on . . . More importantly, I have a son, Nathan, and he's all alone now."

Suddenly powerless before the facts, Rebecca let herself sink into despair: she was dead, it was obvious to her now. At first, she had been relieved that the excruciating pain had gone away, but in retrospect, she regretted having taken the easy way out by letting herself die. She ought to have thought about her son. But there was nothing to be gained by complaining. She was dead and she was afraid, not of having reached the end of her life, but of having left Nathan behind.

Louise tried to console her: it wasn't her fault she had died. She hadn't killed herself, after all.

"It was an accident. You couldn't have prevented it. You have nothing to be angry at yourself for."

Lost in thought, Rebecca was silent now. This troubled Louise, who took Minnie aside.

"Do you think she has a depressive streak?"

"How would I know? I only met her a few minutes ago, just like you."

"Do something to cheer her up. It would be a shame if she left. You know how to make people laugh!"

Minnie wasn't sure she could help this new woman in their midst. She seemed as distant as a statue. What's more, she looked nothing like them with her slim figure and blonde hair that fell loosely around her shoulders. She was even wearing pants! One thing was sure: she was more stricken than the others who came here; she was worrying far too much about this son of hers.

"What will become of Nathan without me?" wondered Rebecca. "I know him inside and out: his silences, his laughing fits, his pet peeves. I can read all his moods. I know he needs two pillows and that he hates to have the bedcovers on top of him. I know his sleepy morning grin that makes me want to hug him, and the way he tries not to smile when he's proud of himself. I'm the only one who can stand that loud Indian music he listens to and who compliments him when he tries to dress nicely, even though he wears the same identical white button-down shirts. I always could find a way to cheer him up."

"He'll learn to take care of himself, don't you worry," said Louise as politely as she could.

"We think we're indispensable," Minnie continued firmly. "But I can assure you that your son will manage very well without you. I saw the same thing happen with my own boys . . ."

Rebecca interrupted her.

"We had a fight the last time I saw him. I told him he'd never amount to anything, and he stormed out without a word."

Louise Cohen was shocked. How could a mother criticize the apple of her eye?

"Just because you never stood up to your Albert didn't make you a better mother," Minnie told her. "I yelled at my boys all the time. They thought I was strict, but they obeyed me. And they thanked me later."

Her remark irritated Rebecca.

"But you didn't die in the middle of an argument with one of them."

"No, I have to admit that would be horrible."

Louise elbowed Minnie. She could be so utterly tactless. This led Minnie to make fun of the "apple of her eye." After all, Louise had hardly shown much consideration for Rebecca herself.

"Maybe if I tell you what happened you'll understand," Rebecca interrupted them. "Nathan's studying law. Not so long ago, he had to take an exam, but he gave up halfway through. He never said a word to me; it was a colleague who told me the story later. When I confronted him, he told me it was none of my business. He said he hated law, that he was only doing it to make me happy, so I could brag about 'my son the lawyer.' He started yelling at me that it was his life and if he felt like failing an exam, that was his business. To think that I had prided myself on the fact that he had been such an easy teenager! 'My life is already ruined and I'm only eighteen and it's all your fault, and that's what matters, not some stupid exam,' he shouted. Now I realize he was right."

"No, no, no! Absolutely not!" Minnie exclaimed. "You knew what was best for him, and that meant taking the exam. He shouldn't have argued with you, and you shouldn't doubt yourself."

"Are you kidding? I was a monster! I looked at him coldly and said how much he had disappointed me, and refused to utter another word. He slammed the door behind him when he left. The accident happened a few hours later."

Louise Cohen was horrified by Rebecca's story. Far worse than her sudden death was the humiliating blow she had dealt her son!

Rebecca continued to talk, oblivious to the disastrous effect she was having on her audience. She felt driven to tell them everything, as if speaking could erase the regrets that were tormenting her.

"I suppose Nathan will feel guilty about my death. He must be telling himself that if he hadn't been so confrontational, I wouldn't have lost my temper . . . and that maybe I could have avoided that stupid accident!"

"Really? Could you have avoided it?"

"No."

Tears filled Rebecca's eyes. Louise took her by the hand and addressed her in a sympathetic tone of voice, even though she was appalled by the younger woman's attitude.

"Now, now. Everything will be fine," she soothed.

Why were these strange women so attentive to her? Rebecca was utterly miserable.

"How do you know? Nathan is an orphan now. I know what he's going through. When my mother died, I was convinced she was there watching me. I used to ask her advice, I shared everything that was happening in my life. I was ten years old and talking to her was a kind of consolation. My father, on the other hand, never spoke of her. He belonged to that generation that never expressed any emotions—to him, complaining was a criminal offense and talking about oneself indecent. Maybe that's why I felt abandoned . . ."

"Nathan won't necessaily have the same reaction as you did," Louise tried to convince her. "Besides, he'll go through a lot of different phases, from despair to sadness to an almost serene nostalgia."

"Albert Cohen never got over your death. In *Book of My Mother*, he begs to see you again, and he does, in his dreams, long after you're gone. Even when you're hiding in a tiny village under a false identity, he feels as close to you as when the two of you lived together. He reproaches you for your selfishness in leaving him; he accuses you of not loving him anymore. And if my calculations are correct, Cohen was forty-four years old when you died. He was an adult and already famous! If he was unable to deal with his grief, imagine what a child like Nathan must be feeling!"

Minnie leaned close to Rebecca:

"Well, try thinking about our feelings! It was just as difficult for us to leave our children behind, to let go, and to realize their lives would go on fine without us. The others will tell you the same thing."

"The others?"

"Oh, you'll see; we aren't the only ones here. There are plenty of mothers: Marcel Proust's, Sigmund Freud's, Romain Gary's . . ."

Rebecca let out a relieved burst of laughter. She was a mother, and she was Jewish. Did that automatically make her the Jewish mother of jokes and stories? Was her presence here among so many famous women proof that her son would be famous someday too?

"Are there only Jewish mothers in this place?"

"Not all Jewish mothers are Jewish," opined Minnie. "Or mothers, either. My husband was a Jewish mother, just like you and me and everyone here. It's an expression, that's all: a synonym for being loving, devoted, heroic, possessive, demanding, paranoid, anxious, unbearable, nosy, and always obsessed with one's children, from their food to their safety."

"So, you're all Jewish too?"

"That's the way it is, don't blame us," said Louise.

Minnie Marx was explaining that the concept of the "Jewish mother" was fairly recent. Starting in the early twentieth century, Jewish mothers were thought to be maternal, protective and loving. That was before American novelists like Saul Bellow and Philip Roth transformed them into "Yiddish mamas" better known for their stifling, even pathological fixation on their children.

"Woody Allen helped on that score, too," Rebecca added.

"Jewish mothers didn't only live in New York City, you know," said Louise Cohen. "Albert wrote *Book of My Mother* in 1954, in France."

Minnie addressed Louise in the gentlest voice she could manage so as not to offend her:

"Jewish mothers have always existed, it's true: Sarah, Rebecca, Rachel, Leah, Jochebed, the mother of Moses . . . As a concept, however, it's an American invention that first became famous in 1964 with Dan Greenberg's book: *How to Be a Jewish Mother*. That changed everything."

"Is Woody Allen's mother here?" asked Rebecca.

"No," replied Louise.

"You've never seen her anywhere?" she insisted.

"Yes, but she didn't stay with us for very long."

"Why? I'm a fan of Woody Allen."

"So am I," agreed Minnie, but she said nothing more on the subject of this missing mother.

Rebecca made a mental note to pursue the conversation later, at least to get some answers. Their explanations were not especially helpful. For the first time, her mind turned to her funeral. How many times had she wondered what it would be like? She could picture her best friend in tears, her colleagues speaking in hushed tones. The movie of her memorial service passed before her eyes. There were people crying, others who just came to sign the register, too rushed or too harried to take an hour out of their schedules. Family and friends surrounded her son. And even if, when she thought about that moment, she always imagined Nathan's father, Anthony, racked with grief, she suspected that in reality he wouldn't come at all. He had left her soon after Nathan's birth and had never become close to his son. Still, she loved the idea of him in mourning because whenever his name came up, her hands shook, her chin trembled, her voice cracked, her heart raced and her thoughts became a jumbled mess. Eighteen years after they had met, she still had the same romantic feelings for him. She lost herself in thought again, imagining her son standing

before the congregation at the synagogue to say a few heartfelt and reas-
suring words about grief and loss.

She was drawn back to her surroundings by Louise.

"Do you have any photos with you?" she wanted to know.

Rebecca reached automatically for her handbag. Her handbag! She
had forgotten its very existence until that moment but, seeing it next to
her, she realized that tired leather purse had become more valuable to her
than her closest friend. Going through its familiar contents made her feel
a little less disoriented. The school photos of Nathan were still there: so
many Nathans, from kindergarten to senior year. If boys tend to look
alike in school photos, Nathan was no exception: neatly parted hair when
he was five, shaggy bangs designed to hide the glasses he hated when he
was ten and a tangle of hair and braces when he was fifteen.

"He's so handsome!" Louise exclaimed when she had looked at them
all. "You must have loved him terribly."

"I adored him! He looks like a Persian miniature with his brown curls
and his almond-shaped eyes."

"With such a blonde mother, he must take after his father," Louise
remarked.

In fact, Nathan resembled Anthony so much that she had often had
difficulty disassociating him from her feelings for his father and treating
him as his own person. Seeing him always filled her with a mix of happiness and heartache, sending her flying from the most genuine admiration
to the sharpest fear that he would never amount to anything.

"Nathan loses his keys all the time, he forgets appointments, he throws
his money away—he would never do a thing if I didn't nag him! His bedroom is such a mess that it's impossible for him to find anything, even if
he wanted to. He's lost without me. When he was little and he struggled to
put on his coat, I did it for him, and I tied his laces too, to spare him the
trouble. I even did his homework instead of explaining it to him."

"You were impatient," suggested Louise. "You didn't want to waste
time."

"It's true. I could never bear delays of any kind. I wanted him to be perfect, but I didn't bother to show him how. Now I'm afraid I raised a good-for-nothing. How will he ever manage without my help?"

"That's what every Jewish mother asks herself," Louise Cohen reassured her.

2

Spoiled Rotten

I was always a child of four to her.

Marcel Proust

And with her hands uplifted and spread out like sunbeams she would bestow on me a priestlike blessing. Then she would give me an almost animal look, vigilant as a lioness, to see if I was still in good health.

Albert Cohen

Louise Cohen was in a mood to chat, so Rebecca decided to indulge her. She wanted some reassurance that she had done a good job raising Nathan and she was curious to find out how the mother of Albert Cohen had made such a talented man of her only son. How had Louise Ferro, the daughter of an Italian lawyer, born in Corfu in 1870, who spoke a Venetian dialect at home, managed to raise a major figure of French literature? Besides the love she clearly bore him, she had no obvious other advantage as far as Rebecca could tell.

"Were you a demanding mother?" Rebecca questioned her. "Did you instill in him a sense of responsibility from a young age?"

"Quite the opposite. I did everything for him. I buttered his toast until he was a teenager. Every single breakfast was an act of love. He was only five when we arrived in Marseille, and I had to leave for work very early in the morning, so I prepared his coffee in a thermos and wrote him a note to button up his coat when it was cold, to wash well, especially behind the ears—it's so easy to forget—to look both ways before crossing the street. I always did my best to sound cheerful because I thought it must be terribly sad to wake up alone in a silent apartment. Sometimes, I even left a photograph of myself on the table: a mere paper companion, but it was something. He must hold the memory dear since he describes our morning ritual in *Book of My Mother*."

"What kind of work did you do?"

"I helped my husband Marco at his shop, 18 rue des Minimes. We lived next door at number 20. I would seize any chance to go see Albert, but it wasn't easy. I never sat down all day; we sold eggs wholesale, and it was backbreaking work. I had to sort them first by weight, then by the date they were laid, which I had to double check by holding each egg up to the light. Then I packed them in straw-lined crates by the dozen, neatly lined up. Then the crates had to be carried out and sent to the clients. It was exhausting."

Minnie Marx tripped over her long skirt and nearly fell on all fours in the middle of the crammed sitting room. There were rugs piled on top of each other, chairs, tables covered with curios and boxes, candlesticks and lamps. Had each of these women brought along her most prized possessions?

"Are you alright? Did you hurt yourself?" Rebecca jumped up.

"Minnie tripped on purpose," observed Louise.

"Why would she do that?"

"To interrupt me, of course."

Rebecca went to help Minnie, who was cursing under her breath:

"That Louise can be so rude! She thinks she's the only person who ever had a hard life, and with only one son. You've seen for yourself now how selfish she is; she doesn't even care if I've twisted my ankle or broken my wrist."

Louise Cohen simply ignored her, steering Rebecca away to tell her all about Albert's childhood.

"Oh, pay me no attention! Really, I'm fine," called a frustrated Minnie after them.

Rebecca had noticed that each of these women seemed to expect her full attention and she felt like a new toy they were fighting over and would eventually discard when the game no longer amused them. She didn't know whom to favor. Louise, for her part, seemed determined to choose for her, and continued her story.

"My boy was smart and serious beyond his years. He made me want to cry. He refused to come home to an empty apartment so he would wait for me on the staircase, in the dark. He knew I'd finally come home to make supper. He made up stories while he waited. That's how he convinced himself that everything he saw around him existed in miniature in his head. If he was at the seashore, he was sure that the Mediterranean was rolling its waves over tiny rocks, with tiny fish and a tiny sun, right in his own head. He created characters for his stories, too. He was always a writer, from his earliest days. Even when we lived in Corfu and he was so small, he saw everything there was to see on that island, that's why he chose it as the setting for his novels."

Whenever she spoke of her son, Louise Cohen's face lit up. Her motherly pride softened her rude and sometimes austere demeanor. Rebecca was fascinated by Corfu and how the family had arrived in Marseille. Besides, she loved nothing better than how childhood stories revealed who a person would become.

Minnie didn't hesitate to interrupt. She'd heard it all a hundred times before.

"Shall I tell you about Dornum?"

"That obscure German village where you were born is of no interest, Minnie. Corfu, on the other hand, is an island bathed in sunlight and honey. Albert named it Cephalonia for his trilogy about the 'Valiant,' where he describes the most beautiful island in the world, fragrant with citrus trees and olive trees. And the sea: 'like an immense crystal that hardly a wave disturbs.' He remembers the perfume of jasmine infused with the saltwater smell. His whole universe is pure poetry."

Louise had Corfu in her blood as she and Albert had lived in harmony with its seasons. They had walked on its beaches, along its fortifications and in its busy streets, "crisscrossed by lines of laundry set to dry in the sun, blue, red, yellow, green . . ." They were inseparable on their island.

"That's enough; I'm leaving you. This bucolic scene is getting on my nerves," announced Minnie, getting to her feet.

"Where will she go?" Rebecca asked Louise.

"She'll be back for dinner, don't worry."

Louise Cohen stretched out full length on the couch as her girlhood memories of Corfu came back to her.

"I never dreamed I was living the happiest years of my life. The Mediterranean climate rocked me, bathed me. I didn't worry about the future. I was just happy having nothing else to do but be a mother. I was so proud of my son: From the day he was born, I was his adoring servant; years later, I would still sometimes get up in the middle of the night to make him marzipan in case he woke up hungry. Albert knew it, too. Didn't he write: 'My mother had no *me*: she had a son'? I was right to go to such lengths to make him happy because he put all those memories—watching me make quince jam or the days he spent home from school sick—into *Book of My Mother*. He cherished every moment we spent together.

It had never occurred to Rebecca that raising a child could be so simple. She could still remember how she worried incessantly over her baby: was he warm enough? Was he breathing normally? Was he bored? Could such an exceptional baby as hers be satisfied with merely eating and sleeping? She couldn't stop obsessing over this child who had never asked to be born. She hardly slept. Like Louise, she would go frequently into his room at night—not to admire him but to reassure herself. She would even wake him to make sure he was alright. He became the center of her universe and he would make her pay for it later.

Nathan must have been twelve years old the night he refused to let her go out on a date. She had put on a pretty dress and was ready to leave, but just as she was closing the door behind her, she heard screaming. Was he making a scene or was he truly frightened? She tried reasoning with him; he cried until he nearly choked. She told him she had the right to live her own life, too, sometimes. He replied in all seriousness that she had sacrificed that right when he was born. She laughed, and she stayed home.

A beautiful, tall woman entered noiselessly.

"Jeanne Proust," Louise murmured. "Just so you know, she's quite a snob."

Marcel Proust's mother was as handsome in person as in her portrait by Anaïs Beauvais: At once forbidding and sensual, with a high forehead, a round face, dark eyes, and a steely gaze that was softened somewhat by a generous chest that a muslin collar only partly concealed. Her gentle voice seemed at odds with the cool elegance she emanated.

"I've come to welcome you. I believe you also have a son who is quite dependent on his mother. Nathan, if I'm not mistaken?"

Rebecca blushed like an adolescent. How could she know that? Seeing the younger woman's embarrassment, Jeanne Proust began to laugh:

"Rest assured; just because we are dead doesn't mean we can read other people's thoughts. I was just outside. I overheard your conversation."

Rebecca felt like a foreigner in a strange land. Intimidated, she wondered if she should shake hands, greet her with a kiss on the cheek, on both cheeks, merely say hello, start a conversation, wait for a verbal cue? She had become accustomed to Louise Cohen and Minnie Marx, so cozily maternal, both of them. Jeanne Proust, on the other hand, was clearly a *grande dame*. Louise broke the uncomfortable silence:

"Jeanne was always worried about Marcel. Much too worried. It made him nervous, the poor child."

"It was his fragile health, ever since he was born," retorted Jeanne, exasperated. "That's why I was on pins and needles every time he became ill: he was such a sickly child. He caught every illness going."

"You were uneasy long before he was born," Louise reminded her.

"Why shouldn't I have been? There was plenty to be anxious about: the war against Prussia, the Commune, the terrible battles, the noise of the bombs and the ruins they left, not to mention the daily hardships we had to endure. I felt frightened and abandoned, far from my parents, despite my frequent visits to them."

"They lived in Auteuil, am I right?" Rebecca asked. "Like you, wasn't Marcel very attached to that house?"

Jeanne's face lit up as she realized Rebecca was a cultivated woman like herself. She would be able to share her most intimate literary moments with her, as well as her boundless admiration for her son's work.

"Marcel spent many weekends there and came often on vacations," she was delighted to confirm for her. "He remembered in particular the long, satin curtains in his bedroom that were an empire blue. Also the little sitting room whose shutters were always kept closed to ward off the day's heat. He wrote about the smell of soap and the 'garishly bourgeois' dining room. Marcel loved that house even though he thought it completely tasteless. We had to get rid of it when my uncle died. That was in February, 1897: such a terribly bitter winter that year the great lawn was entirely frozen."

"It was described in rather more prosaic terms for the purposes of its sale: 'vast house, 1500 square meters with greenhouses and outbuildings, 121 avenue Mozart, with separate entrance 96 rue La Fontaine,'" recited Rebecca. She was rather proud of herself to have remembered the citation.

If there had been a selection process to remain in Jeanne Proust's company, Rebecca would have passed with flying colors. So much so that Louise Cohen felt excluded from the conversation and shared her displeasure with the others:

"Apparently you find Marcel Proust much more interesting than Albert Cohen."

"Not at all."

"You're a terrible liar. I'm going to go find Minnie."

"No! Wait! You were telling me what a mother hen you were to Albert when he was little," she reminded Louise, hoping to lure her back.

"Oh! That was nothing compared to the bond I had with Marcel," Jeanne interrupted. "I never dreamed I would be so moved by his birth. We couldn't have been closer."

Rebecca turned to Louise to encourage her to join in, but she was already long gone.

"Leave her be," Jeanne advised. "We'll see her again later."

Leading her new friend out of the room, Jeanne Proust wanted to know exactly how familiar Rebecca was with Marcel's work. Rebecca hesitated before answering, afraid her knowledge would seem insignificant next to Jeanne's and that she would be asked to leave this strange paradise.

Jeanne had shown her to the winter garden where they settled down in wicker chairs overhung by palm leaves. Everywhere was bougainvillea, oleander, and lemon and orange trees. She was enchanted by it all. Timidly, she framed her answer:

"I have a fair knowledge of his work, but since I arrived here, I think I understand better when your son writes of his separation anxiety. I miss Nathan so much that I can identify with Marcel's despair when you left Venice: everything lost its glow. The water in the canals was suddenly no more than hydrogen and oxygen atoms. The palaces he had admired so greatly before seemed to him just uninteresting piles of marble. Your leaving distorted his whole vision of the world."

"For me, too," said Jeanne Proust. "I was beside myself to think of him all alone. It was around that time that he wrote me these admirable lines: 'When two people like us are so intimately connected, it makes no difference how close together or far apart we may be; we are ever in close communication and always we remain at each other's side.' Isn't that magnificent?"

"That reminds me of his description of the 'Young Ladies of the Telephone' in the *Guermantes Way*, I think. He's speaking to his grandmother—he in Doncières, she in Paris—when he brings up these 'Guardian Angels,' the 'All Powerful by whose intervention the absent rise up at our side, without our being permitted to set eyes on them.'"

Delighted by this reader emeritus, Jeanne pulled a packet of letters from her pocket and handed them to Rebecca, who began to finger through what was an enormous stack of correspondence. Jeanne had insisted that Marcel write her about every last detail of his life, beginning with simple housekeeping. She wanted to stay informed of all his affairs. What needed to be "washed, wiped, inspected, resoled, labeled, darned, embroidered, mended, from collars to buttonholes"? Jeanne wanted to be part of his intimate rituals: what time did he get up and what time did he wash? Had he worked? How long? Did he go out? With whom? She ended one of her letters with this advice: "Be very careful when you are cooking and heating in the evening, I worry about you every night."

"'Be very careful'? You sound like you're addressing a child."

"Marcel was entirely unsuited to practicalities," Jeanne replied defensively.

"Weren't you a bit nosy?" Rebecca wondered out loud, still rifling through the letters. "You left nothing to chance. Even when he was fulfilling his military service, you asked him to date each of his letters and to inform you of his schedule, hour by hour. You seem rather obsessed about his use of time. I wonder if that explains why he finally inverted his biological clock to write at night and sleep during the day?"

"I can't say. We had the same personality, the same jealousy, the same possessiveness and worry. He led a very disordered life but he still needed to kiss me goodnight in order to sleep."

"It's not so uncommon as you think," interrupted Louise Cohen, who had found them again.

"Oh! Louise!" Rebecca was startled by every "apparition" of these silently moving women.

"Albert wrote about my bedtime kisses and stories, too. There's not a mother in the world who doesn't kiss her child goodnight," Louise remarked.

"Well, it was different for me," Jeanne Proust assured her. "It pained me terribly to leave him. Every night before he fell asleep, while he tossed and turned in his bed, I would wait stock-still in the hallway between our bedrooms, listening to his every breath."

"'For a long time I used to go to bed early,'" Rebecca said, reciting from memory the famous first line of *Remembrance of Things Past*. "His night fears must have been very powerful since he begins the novel with them."

"He described that same scene on five different occasions in his books," Jeanne revealed proudly.

"The kiss scene is mentioned five times?"

Jeanne was emphatic in her response:

"In each version, Marcel describes the intolerable absence of his mother. She abandons him in his room to a night that seems endless. If she is in the house entertaining guests, he waits in vain for her to return. If she is going out for the evening, she leaves him alone. That she had a life of her own was unbearable."

"Could we look at a few of his books?" Rebecca asked.

"You don't believe me?" Jeanne replied.

Rebecca couldn't think how to explain her need to verify Jeanne's claims in the texts. Professional force of habit, she concluded.

"I do believe you," Rebecca insisted. "I like to read, that's all."

So as not to offend Jeanne, she decided to appease her by asking her to tell the different versions of the night kiss.

Thrilled to have found someone who so clearly appreciated her son's work, she began.

"None of the scenes are quite the same. The most famous passage is in *Swann's Way*, where he describes the evening when Swann comes to dinner. In *Jean Santeuil*, it's Professor Surlande, the doctor, who is the guest. In both cases, Marcel knows there is company that evening and that he must stay in his room, but he is terrified by the coming night and he is desperate for some way to call me—I mean, the Narrator's mother—back to him. Would I come say goodnight, kiss him a last time? The passage revolves around that essential question, and Marcel creates an almost palpable level of suspense."

"It couldn't have been easy; he digresses so," said Louise.

Unperturbed by her sarcasm, Jeanne continued.

"As the mother mounts the stairs, Marcel slips out of his room. Surprised, petrified, she stares at him: what is he doing in the hall? What will her husband do if he discovers them there? She's afraid he will disapprove of her helping her son back into bed. On the other hand, it would be cruel to leave him trembling there on the threshold."

She turned to Rebecca.

"Do parents still believe that it's necessary to treat children harshly to prepare them for adulthood?"

"It's a subject of debate," Rebecca offered, putting together a longer answer in her head, about Baby Boomers, pampered children, the flip-flopping of certain psychologists on the question, but Jeanne interrupted her thoughts.

"In *Jean Santeuil*, the Narrator's mother explains to Surlande that an excess of affection spoils a child; he should be drilled into shape instead. She wants to break her son of his 'little girl habits' and so she does not return to his room."

"Is that what you thought, too?"

"My husband was a great proponent of a 'manly' education, but not me. It made me sick to obey Adrien, but sometimes I did. If I could have, I would have slept in my son's room every night. Marcel wrote that his one consolation was that I would come to kiss him goodnight, but he also describes how painful that moment was for him, because it was too brief; I would have to leave him again. I had no wish to inflict that pain on him."

"So you tried to reason with him."

"What else could I do? Marcel knew how much it upset me to be called back to him again and again, and that his fits interfered with the education I was trying to instill in him. Knowing this was not enough to prevent him from doing it, however. Sometimes, out of the blue, his father suggested that I go to him. He describes such a scene in *Swann's Way*."

"That's incredible!" Rebecca burst out. "You were strict when his father would have been lenient because he understood how frightened his child was. You're the one who comes off as inflexible."

"How dare you criticize me that way!" Jeanne shot back, furious.

"She's sensitive," Louise Cohen whispered.

Feeling guilty now, Rebecca excused herself.

"I'm really not one to judge. Nathan stuck to me like glue. He used to call me all the time. I couldn't eat lunch without him interrupting, more than once too. My work colleagues would always complain. He'd ask for advice on everything: what to eat for lunch, what time to leave to catch a train. He wouldn't hesitate to send me a text when I was in the middle of teaching, with the most trivial questions, but they were paralyzing for him. The more ridiculous the question, the more he needed help deciding. And I always answered him."

Lost in thought about Nathan, Rebecca hadn't noticed that the others had left. Had she been talking to herself? Where had they disappeared to? She had probably scared them away with her talk of texting. How could she not have heard them leave? Someone had brought in a very elegant porcelain tea service. Who? Did it matter? Alone for the first time, Rebecca let her mind wander. Had she, like Jeanne Proust, raised a son who was unable to live without his mother? Hadn't she, too, encouraged his dependence? A wave of anxiety washed over her. Hoping for distraction, she walked, reciting poems to herself. Verlaine always soothed her in times of crisis, like a beautiful painting or a magnificent landscape.

She came to a library so enormous she couldn't help comparing it to Alexandria's before it went up in flames. There were hundreds of thousands of books, on shelves as far as the eye could see. If she had ever wondered what heaven might be like, she couldn't have asked for more; this was her kind of paradise. She chose a volume of poetry and began to read, but oddly enough, Verlaine's verses didn't move her. She tried Rimbaud, Apollinaire, Baudelaire and even a few of her favorite fables by La Fontaine; they left her absolutely indifferent. Even Eluard had no effect whatsoever. Page after page only bored her to death. (She found the expression a strange one in her present context!) The poems she loved best of all seemed dull, insipid even, and far less interesting, certainly, than her own life—which was no more. She was eaten up by the thought that she had failed to raised Nathan properly. No one could accuse her of being careless with his education, but she had gone about it alone: no models, no references. Here, surrounded by these different examples of maternal love, it seemed to her that everything would have been different if she had had a mother. Brooding over the question, she could not bring herself to read. So she was relieved to see Jeanne come in and begin searching for a book . . . by Proust, on one of the shelves.

"I'm disturbing you," Jeanne excused herself.

"Not at all; I'm not reading. I was thinking about a mother's role and how complicated it is. I was wondering whether we are the same parents to our children as our parents were to us, or whether the opposite is true, which comes to the same thing. You were talking about your emotional attachment to Marcel, but what kind of a relationship did you have with your mother?"

"I adored her. We were so very close. Everything she knew and loved, she passed on to me: Beethoven, Saint-Simon's *Memoirs*, Madame de Sévigné's *Letters*, the basics of piano, as well as Latin, English and German. Culture was of the utmost importance to her, and for me, too. I admit that I did precisely the same thing for Marcel that my mother did for me."

"Let's go find the others."

Jeanne led Rebecca back into the living room. There was no one to be found, but a grey shawl was draped over a sagging armchair, a shoe had been forgotten in the middle of the floor, and a barely-touched box of chocolates lay suggestively open. It was hard not to notice that Rebecca's new companions didn't exactly share her maniacal attention to order. The slightest mess was enough to wake her up in the middle of the night; everything had to be in its place by the time she switched off her bedside light. Jeanne, on the other hand, didn't seem bothered in the least. On the contrary, sitting perfectly erect on a chair, she looked like a duchess as she motioned to Rebecca to make herself comfortable on the sofa. She began to tell the story of her brother, a respected lawyer and a bachelor until the age of forty-four. Their mother never lived to see him marry. Devoted as he was to her, he probably would have never taken a wife if Adèle hadn't decided one day to breathe her last. She was an exemplary mother who declared her love to her daughter in impassioned letters, rather like Madame de Sévigné. But she could be extremely strict, too. Jeanne had written to Marcel once: "I know one other mother who is nothing compared to her children, who *transfers* herself entirely to them."

"Madame de Sévigné was so invasive a mother that the poor girl had to run clear to the other side of France to get away from her," Rebecca observed. "Contrary to what people may think, it was not a happy relationship but an abusive one."

"She was a Jewish mother and she didn't even know it," Louise Cohen put in, as she settled herself next to Rebecca, supporting her back with a cushion.

Rebecca was becoming accustomed to the women's unexpected comings and goings and didn't even blink this time. She was on a favorite topic now.

"Madame de Sévigné was demanding, intelligent and always made her presence felt. My own mother was the same," Jeanne remarked.

"She must have been a terror, just like me; I always did too much for Albert," Louise Cohen said.

"Mothers are always held accountable for everything that goes wrong," Jeanne continued. "If we're absent, it's scandalous. If we're too present, it's unbearable. Yet no one seems to understand that it's the force of our love that drives us to constantly intervene. Even Marcel struggled with that; he has Madame de Villeparisis chastise Madame de Sévigné for the exaggerated way she worries over her daughter."

"And you interpret that as a criticism of yourself?" Rebecca asked, horrified by Jeanne's narcissism. She evidently had read all of Marcel's books but only with an eye to herself. Was the love Marcel bore her the only interesting part of *Remembrance of Things Past*? Was the reason she turned her gaze so frequently to it so she could find her reflection in its pages?

"You can make fun of me all you want, I couldn't care in the least," said Jeanne angrily.

"You aren't the only overbearing mother," countered Louise Cohen. "Rebecca, I'm sure you've read *Portnoy's Complaint*, by Philip Roth. I discovered it here in this library and I come back to it again and again."

"Did you want to talk about Sophie Portnoy? She's a horribly possessive mother."

"And so intrusive that her son, Alex, becomes convinced that every one of his teachers is his mother in disguise and that she has superhuman powers because she's always back in the kitchen when he arrives home from school. Every day, he wonders if he'll walk in the door and surprise her before she has time to change back into herself. It's a fantasy he never outgrows; he believes steadfastly in the omnipotence of his mother."

"Sophie Portnoy is a character in a novel," Jeanne reminded them, not bothering to hide her disdain.

"Roth must have found inspiration somewhere," replied Rebecca. "Nothing is complete fiction. Have you ever seen Woody Allen's movie, *Oedipus Wrecks*? It's a short film in the *New York Stories* trilogy—Scorsese and Coppola made the other two. Woody Allen has this dream that he's driving a hearse with his mother in the coffin, but even though she's dead, she's still criticizing his driving, complaining that if he doesn't slow down, she won't go to the cemetery. So he does, and for the rest of the ride she's giving him directions how to get there."

"I've never seen it," said Louise.

Rebecca was surprised to hear herself use her lecture hall voice to explain how Mrs. Millestein watched over her son.

"Her garishly made-up face, lined with wrinkles and crowned by a lavender-colored permanent wave, appears in the clouds. She begins to ask everyone in the street if her son's behaving himself. She has photos of Sheldon to prove that he was once an adorable little boy. But Sheldon is in his fifties now and can't hide from her, not even in his own apartment, because she's peering in at him through the window. He doesn't have a moment of respite; nothing escapes her. She's more all-knowing than God."

"Nettie didn't like that movie very much; such a caricature of her," mused Jeanne.

"I can certainly understand her reaction. Where is she? I'd love to meet her."

"Perhaps she's still in one of those clouds, watching her son like in the film," wondered Louise.

"Impossible," Jeanne replied, exasperated.

"It's been ages since we've seen her," Louise observed.

"Why did she leave?" Rebecca still wanted to know.

"I think she found our company tiresome. All she ever wanted to talk about was Woody-this, Woody-that—his life, his movies, his childhood, every single stage of his development . . ."

Rebecca had already gotten the feeling Nettie wasn't the only son-obsessed mother in this heaven. But what if Rebecca was to blame for getting the others started? She had hardly given them much choice with her questions, traumatized as she was by her sudden separation from Nathan. She had to admit she also wanted to feel close to these mothers whose sons where the only men that mattered in their lives. It was so refreshing to hear the stories of famous men told by their mothers.

3

Husbands and Fathers

Jeanne Proust had changed into a magnificent black dress with a bustle in back that showed off her slim waist and from which a cascade of silk fell to her ankles.

"How elegant you are!" Rebecca cried, noting also her buttoned boots and the white flower she had slipped into her chignon.

"Marcel could not have agreed less with you. He detested this style of dress. His female characters are always in flowing gowns; Anne Swann and the Duchess of Guermantes wear silk muslin and every kind of gauzy, fluid fabric, in mauve, violet and lavender . . ."

"Did he ever express an opinion about how you dressed?"

"It would have been hard for him, my poor dear; I changed several times a day. My husband couldn't stand slovenliness."

"Why is it none of your husbands are with you?" asked Rebecca.

"I don't know why but I won't complain; it was difficult enough when we lived together. Adrien intimidated me, and I didn't dare speak to him. In any case, I rarely saw him, as he was always absorbed by his work. He was chief physician at the Lariboisière Hospital and traveled frequently. When he was home, he often went out without me. We never understood each other, I'm afraid. Even our apartment on the Boulevard Malesherbes, where we lived for over twenty years didn't suit either of us. I worked hard to make it comfortable but it was too luxurious for Adrien, who hardly spent any time there, and despite all my efforts to refurnish it, I never felt at home in it myself.

Rebecca supposed it had been an arranged marriage, in keeping with the times. Jeanne Proust was telling her, in fact, that she had refused several suitors and that she was already twenty-one years old when she married Adrien Proust, a famous doctor and fifteen years her senior. He had first set his sights on joining the seminary, so he had never sought a wife before he met her. The son of a modest Catholic grocer, he was brilliant and hard-working. His parents were not happy to see him marry a Jew, no matter how rich she was. But Adrien was ambitious. He married Jeanne for her money and her contacts. Jeanne's father, on the other hand, the powerful and respected Nathé Weil, had chosen a young man who suited his ambitions: a Catholic, with a promising career, who would open more doors of Parisian society for his daughter, as many upper middle class Jewish families aspired to do. As for Jeanne's mother, she thought her future son-in-law was a handsome man. Did Jeanne have any say in the matter? Describing the parents of Jean Santeuil, Proust wrote that a marriage of love was pure vice. Love followed marriage, and not vice versa; it was a commonly held opinion. "No woman ever stopped loving her husband any more than she would have stopped loving her mother," Proust had written.

"It would have pleased me if Adrien had tried to close the distance that I had created between us," Jeanne was saying. "But he never did. It wasn't a question of religion; we were divided both by culture and personality. We weren't married in the Church and I never converted, but since I was an agnostic and he was an atheist, religion was never a source of conflict. On the other hand, he thought it was a waste of time to read anything but newspapers and on the rare occasions he forced himself to accompany me to a concert, he invariably fell asleep. Museums were even worse; he had no patience for art whatsoever. I wasn't offended. He was my intellectual superior but we did not share the same tastes. So I instilled in Marcel all the culture that Adrien lacked."

She fell silent, her gaze locked on something only she could see. A memory of Marcel, doubtless.

"Didn't you have anything in common with your husband? What did you talk about?" Rebecca wanted to know.

"The children, of course, and household affairs. We had a large domestic staff to oversee, because we hosted parties so frequently; I loved being the mistress of the house! I was always available when he came home from the office or his travels. We had been married little more than a year when Marcel was born, as I told you. His birth changed everything."

"You mean you chose to be Marcel's mother rather than Adrian's wife."

"Chose? I'm not sure about that. Marcel was so fragile and in such distress that he needed me far more than my husband. I often wondered if Adrien was unfaithful because I spent too much time with Marcel or because he wasn't satisfied with me."

Rebecca was at pains to understand how Jeanne could speak so objectively of her husband's extramarital affairs. Had she never been possessive or jealous? How could she tolerate his adultery? Were appearances more important than anything else in Jeanne Proust's day?

"Having a mistress in full view of society was proof that the country doctor had established himself in high society," Jeanne explained with the same serenity. "It was thanks to me that he became an elegant Parisian."

Rebecca could think of nothing to say in reply.

"Does that shock you?"

The voice that had calmly asked the question was one Rebecca had never heard before. She turned around to discover a slim, willowy figure—Amalia Freud. Once again, Rebecca felt the shock of meeting a new woman here. She looked her over carefully; under a thick crown of black braids she had a ravishing, perfectly oval face and a curious gaze that held Rebecca with an embarrassing intensity. She was wearing a long dress in black taffeta covered by a white guipure. It seemed to Rebecca that such a display of elegance had to be a joke of some kind.

She was about to say something when the others broke in: it was time for lunch and everyone was dying of hunger!

"But it's not ready!" Amalia Freud protested.

She turned to Rebecca and began to describe what marriage was like in the late 19th century: a social and religious institution that guaranteed the development of families. Love had nothing to do with it.

"Marcel got one thing right at least."

"One thing, really?" shot back Jeanne.

Amalia didn't bother responding. Each was the other's equal: beautiful and cultivated, they were both heavyweights.

"As Jacob's third wife, I can tell you he had great success with women," Amalia Freud continued. "There's nothing to wonder about there: he looked just like Sigmund. With his almond-shaped eyes and his piercing look, he had such charm, such charisma, and he knew how to use them with women. But as for caring whether or not he was unfaithful to me, it would have been a waste of time! I could have done nothing about it so I didn't even ask myself the question."

Amalia Freud was born Amalia Nathanson in 1835 in Brody, a small town in the northeast of Galicia, near the Russian border. She was very close to her parents, who moved the family next to Odessa, and then to Vienna. Middle class, her father earned a good living as a salesman, just like her four brothers, the two oldest of whom lived in Odessa also. Julius was born two years after Amalia but died of tuberculosis when he was twenty. The third child of the family became a lawyer in Krakow. Even as a girl, Amalia had a strong personality. Why did such a pretty, radiant, cultivated and confident seventeen year old marry Jacob Freud, a man twenty years her senior, who had two sons from a first marriage and who had just lost his second wife? His position as a wool merchant could not have swept her off her feet.

"We were married on July 29, 1855, in Vienna, and I was happy that day."

"But why did you marry him?" Rebecca insisted.

"In the early years of our marriage, I was impressed by this jovial and amusing man."

"And you had eight children."

"I certainly wasn't going to shirk my conjugal duties."

"And you didn't love him?"

No one had seen the tiny Louise Cohen enter the room. She elbowed Rebecca so sharply the younger woman only barely suppressed a cry of pain.

"Stop interrogating her," she whispered.

Why was Louise so careful about Amalia's feelings when she wasn't the least bit bothered by Rebecca's questions? Amalia answered her: the fact that she didn't love her husband made no difference.

"It took me some time to admit it: I had so many other worries. Jacob was a terrible businessman and we kept moving house, under the pretense that business would be better elsewhere, but it never was. He was used to living off other people's generosity. My parents tried to help us, then his own sons, when they moved to England."

"Did you blame him for your poverty?" said Rebecca.

"We lived in the poorest neighborhood of Vienna where the main wave of immigrants had settled: Bohemians, Moravians, Hungarians, Ruthenians and Croatians. With so much immigration, Vienna was a cosmopolitan city that spoke many languages and it was the most Jewish city after Warsaw, but also the most expensive. My own family lived in the same apartment throughout my childhood, but as a married woman, I never stopped moving. First we went to Jacob's parents, but that became unbearable with three children. Then we went to shared housing, where we had to trace a line around our private space in the common room. As difficult as that was, it was better than having to live off his family. With Jacob,

I discovered a level of subsistence I could never have imagined. And I was terrified of dying. In 1897, for every thousand residents in Vienna, seventy died of tuberculosis. My brother died of it, but I survived. To answer you frankly, no, I didn't blame Jacob for our poverty, only his lack of will. None of his plans ever materialized but he never stopped believing in them; even after he stopped working as a wool merchant he continued to pass himself off as one because he could never admit to himself that he was only a clerk to immigrants. We lived perpetually on the edge of ruin. The worst was in 1865: Josef, Jacob's brother, was arrested for possession of counterfeit bank bills. Just imagine my shame! It was in the newspapers of course, and living as we did in the Jewish quarter where everyone knew each other, we were the object of remarks, from sympathy to scorn to insult."

"Lunch is served!" Minnie Marx's voice boomed over Amalia's last words. Minnie took food very seriously and she began urging everyone into the heavy, wood-paneled dining room, whose gloomy dark green curtains had seen better days. It reminded Rebecca of one of those over-stuffed 19th century houses such as Vuillard painted. The women took their accustomed places around the table, with Rebecca seated between Minnie Marx and Amalia Freud, who continued her story.

"You can look it up if you like, Rebecca. It's in the report the police submitted to the Foreign Ministry on October 16, 1865: 'On 20 June of the present year, the Israelite Josef Freud was apprehended as he was preparing to sell a large quantity of counterfeited bank bills, precisely 359 forged bills of fifty rubles each.' The worst was that Jacob's adult sons were accused as well: 'The veritable source of the counterfeit bills is in England.' My stepsons were living in Manchester at the time. In one of these letters, it says they had 'as much money as the sand on the seashore' and that 'as intelligent, sensible and prudent as they are, it won't be long before they make a fortune.'"

"It wasn't Jacob's fault," Rebecca comforted her. "He must have been as upset as you were."

"Of course, but instead of fighting the accusations and trying to help his sons, he just moaned and groaned. Almost overnight his hair turned grey. Luckily, the police report confirmed his sons' innocence."

The women were now passing a platter of veal stew with rice. Rebecca hardly noticed, so fascinated was she by the story of the Freud brothers. She returned to her line of questioning.

"Were your stepsons involved with Josef? Were they guilty of any wrongdoing?"

"Jacob suspected they must have been. They were originally from Tysmenitz; perhaps they had stayed in touch with some Polish insurgents who were fighting for autonomy in that part of the former Polish kingdom that was occupied by Russia in those days. That would be one thing, but counterfeiting money is entirely something else. In any case, there was no proof and they were never implicated. But Josef and his accomplice were sentenced to ten years in prison."

"I imagine Jacob was a good father, judging from the respect Freud always showed him."

"It's true that Jacob appears more often in his books than I do, his own mother. I never understood why Jacob was so tough on the children and such an absent father, but Sigi adored him just the same. He always made excuses for his incompetence. As soon as Sigi figured out that Jacob couldn't afford to pay for his studies, he learned to take care of himself and never complained. Joseph Breuer used to lend him money for his day-to-day needs, what's more, he opened his home to him as if he were his own son and introduced him to his many clients, including the famous Anna O., who gave him the idea of the cathartic method. Sigi was good at finding surrogate fathers and he never asked himself why."

Fascinated by Amalia, Rebecca hardly touched her plate, but she wasn't really hungry. Minnie Marx stuffed her face just like the permanently starved Harpo, who never stopped taking small mouthfuls and signaled each new bite with a tap on his plate. Louise ate slowly. As for Amalia Freud, as soon as she stopped speaking, she threw herself upon her food as if she didn't know where her next meal would come from.

"Did your other children get much attention from your husband?" Rebecca asked Amalia Freud.

"He was a wonderful father to our five daughters. But he was feeling old by the time Alexander was born, ten years after Sigi."

"Did you fight?"

"Rarely. It wasn't Jacob's fault he exasperated me. I avoided him as much as I could and that was quite a feat in those tiny apartments we lived in. I had a very rich interior life and I spent all my love on Sigi."

"You stayed in a marriage with a man you didn't love for forty years?"

"Fortunately, Jacob died when I was sixty. It felt like my life had finally begun. My marriage had only been an interruption. You can't imagine the pleasure of no longer having a husband: I woke up every morning with a smile on my face, stretching out in the bed that at last I had all to myself."

It suddenly occurred to Rebecca that perhaps she had been wrong to regret her life as a single mother. She had never wanted to fall madly in love. In fact, her responsibilities toward Nathan were sufficient for her to rule out anything that crazy. But she had longed for a man in her bed. She had been seduced by colleagues over the years, and had even made a habit of seeking out the foreign ones, not only because she thought any accent was sexy, but also because the affair could only last as long as his one-year visa. Frenchmen, on the other hand, were off limits; they never failed to fall hopelessly in love and she hated ending a relationship. Her ideal man was gentle, willing and part-time. But an ideal man was too hard to find, she told herself, and decided to stay single.

She was so deep in thought that she didn't notice when a wrinkled, grey-haired woman sat down next to her and extended a firm handshake.

"I'm Roman Gary's mother," the woman introduced herself.

Rebecca thought it an odd introduction; had she no other identity than that of a mother? She looked over the famous Mina. The heroine of *Promise at Dawn* was a tired old woman. In fact, she looked as if she had spent her entire life in a labor camp or on a chain gang. Rebecca searched her professional memory for anything she'd ever learned about Roman Gary's mother. The name Owczynska floated back to her. Mina's maiden name, she concluded, wondering why it was always the most insignificant details that stuck with her. Mina was also very beautiful, however, and a bit wild: a passionate romantic who loved the theater and dreamed of adventure.

"I left home when I was sixteen," Mina was saying. "Before my parents could marry me off. I wanted to fall in love. I was a rebel, always up in arms about something and ready to take any risk to get away. You'd understand if you'd known what life was like in Swieciany, a little village of woodcutters in what was still Russia then. I came from a family of Orthodox Jews who were grocers and grain merchants and weavers, traditional occupations for us. It was a close-knit community; everyone knew each other's business. Nothing and no one could have kept me there."

"Where did you go?"

"Moscow. I joined a group of itinerant actors who traveled all over Russia. We played in castles and barns and village squares. For the first time in my life, I felt free. I had so many roles. There was Maria Antonovna, the abandoned daughter of the Mayor in Gogol's *The Government Inspector*, and Ekaterina, in *The Storm* by Ostrovsky; she leaves her disappointing husband the first chance she has to run off with a certain Boris, but he turns out to be no great catch either and she ends up committing suicide. I only played strong women, and with great passion. I was excessively happy, I sang, I danced, I lived. And then, one day, I had to go back . . . to get married. My first husband was detestable."

A wracking cough broke off her story. She looked exhausted. Jeanne Proust poured her a glass of water and signaled to Rebecca that she needed help with the dessert. In the kitchen, they found a platter already laden with fruits of all kinds of seasons and regions: papayas, litchi, mangoes, grapes, oranges, pears, cherries, peaches . . .

"Where did all this fruit come from? Who does the cooking?" wondered Rebecca out loud.

"Don't bother with such trivial matters," Jeanne ordered her in reply. "I had to warn you not to be taken in by Mina's stories. A great actress! She was in a troupe of pure amateurs."

"That doesn't change the fact that she lived an exciting life." Rebecca knew only that Mina had remarried when she was thirty-three, to Arieh Leib Kacew, who was four years her junior. She didn't know how they had met. Was this second marriage arranged by her parents? Was Arieh madly in love with Mina? Did he brave a scandal by marrying an older woman, a divorcée? However their relationship had begun, Rebecca wanted to believe that Arieh loved her and that he tried to make her happy. No easy task with such an adventuress whose thirst for fame and freedom was probably insatiable. It was hard to imagine her and her outsized ego living in her father-in-law's house, as Jewish tradition dictated, in the decrepit Jewish quarter of Vilnius with its pogroms and hardships. The Kacew were a lower-middle-class Russian family of furriers. Those couldn't have been happy years for Mina. Her life changed on May 21, 1914, however, when her son Roman Kacew was born. He would become Romain Gary, and nothing would ever be the same again.

Back in the dining room, Mina was eating cherries rather mechanically, but the color was coming back into her cheeks.

"Gary hardly mentions his father," Rebecca remarked. "Did he live with you?"

"Why do you bring him up? Romain is a far more interesting topic of conversation."

For a moment, she continued to pop cherry after cherry into her mouth. She couldn't stand silence, however, and since no one else seemed willing to keep the conversation going, she decided to answer Rebecca.

"Well, if you must know, Arieh was called up into the army during World War I. Romain was four when he came home, but he left us again for a much younger woman who bore him two children ten years later. I was hurt, humiliated. But, I think . . . When I look back at it all now, I think that was exactly what I wanted. Exactly! I think I wanted to be left alone with my little boy. Romain filled me with joy. So many times I would ask him to turn his head toward the light so I could drink in his magnificent blue eyes. That was all I needed to feel happy."

"So, Romain took the place of your husband."

"You could say that. I did everything in my power for him, just like a wife hoping to further her husband's career. I'll tell you a story so you can see exactly what I mean. One day, it occurred to me that, without any means to pay for lessons, my adored son would never learn to play tennis, so I went to the imperial park of Nice and marched right out onto the courts to explain that with just a little training, my son would become a champion. He had to get in free!"

"He must have been a real natural talent." Rebecca concluded.

"Not at all. He was a clumsy player at best. He'd never done more than hit a few balls. But I could never admit that; no one would have taken me seriously. The club manager tried to reason with me to lower my voice, especially since King Gustave of Sweden was there at that moment. The poor man: he obviously didn't know me. I went right up to the king, who was taking his tea on the lawn. I remember he was an older man, very elegant in his straw hat, sitting under a white parasol. I told him how wonderful my Romain was: The future French champion, and he was only fourteen! The king wasn't the least bit surprised to hear it and he invited my son to show him what he could do with his trainer. The rest of the story is less glorious. All I can say is that Romain did his best. He describes how humiliating the experience was in *Promise at Dawn*: 'I jumped, dived, bounced, pirouetted, ran, fell, bounced up again, flew through the air [. . .] but the most I can say is that I did, just once, touch the ball.' No matter: The King of Sweden was so impressed by his courage that he paid Romain's fees. We never set foot there again but I had done what I set out to do."

"You always believed in miracles," said Louise Cohen.

"I did just the same for my own boys," agreed Minnie Marx. "Did I tell you how I managed to get reimbursed for Harpo's harp at twice the price I paid for it?"

" Minnie, you've told that story a hundred times already," said Louise wearily.

"There was a train accident, and I was threatening the conductor that I would send for the insurance agent," Minnie began anyway.

"Minnie, it's my turn. I was in the middle of telling the story of my life."

"Or maybe Romain's?" Rebecca suggested.

"What's the difference? I lived with him."

"If you were exactly the same, how did you manage to raise him?" Rebecca asked.

"He owed me his respect, and I insisted that he always come to my defense," Mina explained by way of an answer. "Any time I felt insulted, I ordered him to slap the person who had wronged me. I knew I could count on him; he even went in my place to see the shopkeepers when they were looking to be paid. I was often in debt, with no means to pay anyone back. But I had nothing to worry about: Romain protected me as well as any man."

"He was your Prince Charming. Is that why you never remarried?"

"Twice is plenty. Of course, I didn't lack for offers."

This reminded Mina of the story of Zaremba. He was a painter staying at the Mermonts' boarding house who was so impressed by Mina's adoration of her son that he asked to marry her, hoping she would love him just as unconditionally.

"Zaremba asked Romain for my hand in marriage, and he accepted. My son wanted me to marry him. He thought my devotion to his education was ruining my life. How could he think such a thing? Romain was my greatest success! Thanks to him, my life was worth something: He became famous! I always knew he would, even when he was a child. Our cleaning lady, Mariette, knew it too. At first she thought I sang his praises because he was my son but then she started to wonder. Maybe there was something special about him after all?"

"What did you tell the painter who was in love with you?"

"I sent him back to Poland, and that was my last and final suitor."

"Come with me, Rebecca. I'd like to get an apple," Jeanne Proust interrupted.

Minnie held one out to her, but Jeanne, who was already on her feet, brushed her aside and motioned to Rebecca to follow her. As soon as they were in the kitchen, she exploded in anger: Mina was an utter liar, all her stories came from Gary's novels, Zaremba was a character in *Promise at Dawn*, and he was modeled on Philippe Maliavien, a Russian painter who lived in a castle outside Nice. Even the name Zaremba was stolen from an 18th century Lithuanian myth. Gary couldn't stand to see his mother old and sick so he made up the story. How could she tell such whoppers?

"Whatever truth there is, it certainly demonstrates the kind of relationship she had with her son."

"Why are you defending her? What do you know about it?"

"Nothing, but it reminds me of something I went through."

"Oh! In that case, tell me everything. I adore a love story."

Rebecca had fallen for a Russian literature professor. Unlike her other foreign lovers, he had no plans to return to his native country and she had gotten in over her head. For one thing, he looked like the hero of a Russian novel: Alexis Vronski, Nicolas Rostov, Youri Jivago . . . He was going to move in with her and Nathan, and the night of the move, she and the professor were going out for a celebratory dinner. Nathan must have been ten years old at the time and she was giving him a few instructions. She wrote down her cell-phone number, reminded him to brush his teeth and told him he could watch some television, a huge concession for her. She must have told him fifty times how much she loved him. Nevertheless, by the time she got home, Nathan was passed out. At the hospital, they told her he had drunk himself into a coma. Had he tried to commit suicide? In any case, that was the end of her Russian love affair.

"You never saw him again?"

"Not after the hospital, no."

"And Nathan, what did he say afterwards?"

"Nothing, ever. He was ashamed, the poor darling, but it was me who was guilty."

"Don't you think you're jumping to conclusions?" Jeanne prompted her gently. "Isn't it possible that Nathan just made a mistake, that he took advantage of being alone in the house to drink for the first time? Many children who are smothered with attention act out in these ways."

Rebecca blanched: The idea had never occurred to her.

"Was I a fool? It took me a long time to get over him. I cried all the time and I became even stricter with Nathan, without even realizing it. I was obviously angry at him. Did I make a terrible mistake?"

"There's no point in crying over spilled milk," Jeanne said. "What's done is done."

Jeanne was tired. She had no patience for other peoples' troubles, and Mina had gotten on her nerves.

"You don't have to go back into the dining room, Rebecca."

"What if Mina is expecting us?"

Jeanne just shrugged her shoulders and went her way.

In fact, everyone had gotten up from the table, so Rebecca went looking for Mina. Instead she came across Louise Cohen, who was riding on a breeze of jasmine in a Mediterranean garden, stretched out in a hammock suspended between two olive trees. Rebecca followed her lead and lay down in a chaise longue, watching the birds flit back and forth as a lone cloud asserted itself against the cobalt sky.

Blushing slightly and looking a little tipsy, Louise broke into the story of her love life.

"I loved my husband and my son both. I was eighteen when I married Marco. I had only admiration for him. I remember, it was December 25, 1875. We were in Corfu, and the sky was a deep sea blue. I didn't love him at first but I agreed to marry him. Ten months later, Albert Abraham Caliman was born. I lived for the next six years with my in-laws. Marco's father was president of the Hebrew community. He was always good to me, better than to Marco with whom he fought constantly. They worked together at the family soap factory and they never agreed on anything. Abraham wasn't an easy man and he refused to listen to his son's advice on how to modernize the business and diversify their soaps, with perfumes and new shapes. He would fly into a rage and call him an idiot. He didn't see that the economic crisis was going to change everything in Corfu and stir up anti-Semitism. For him, Marco was always wrong. He crushed Marco, who never got over it."

"Albert wrote about his father's severity and how you both were afraid of him."

"Marco followed his father's example: authoritarian and violent. He was the same father to Albert as his father was to him, and I spent my time protecting my darling from him."

"Were you frightened of Marco, too?"

"That's what Albert thought. He says so in *Book of My Mother*."

"But what did you think?" Rebecca insisted.

"I hated it when he drank but I always managed to calm him down or reason with him. I would cajole or flatter him; it soothed him. Never underestimate the power of a woman."

"You were the stronger one."

"But I could never let him know that. He would have been furious. My main concern was Albert, so I did what I had to so he would leave us in peace. I had the same intense relationship with Albert as Jeanne Proust and Mina Kacew had with their sons."

It occurred to Rebecca that Louise Cohen's proclaimed love for her brutal husband was a facade; she was an abusive mother, just like the others, who kept her husband away from her child. He was no more involved in his son's upbringing than Adrien Proust and Arieh Kacew had been with theirs.

"Tell me, Louise: did Marco's violence influence Albert's theory of the ridiculous male?"

"I've wondered about that, too," Louise confessed timidly. "He wrote with disdain about those men who are so enamored of their strength but who never impress anyone other than a few 'prehistoric' women who will unconditionally follow their 'Neanderthal men'. He could never forgive the women who loved those baboons. I think he looked down on me too for loving Marco."

Mina appeared in the garden, wearing a light dress, her hair tinted that shade of mauve so characteristic of elderly ladies who try to hide their grey hair.

"Romain Gary also exalted femininity, its gentleness and compassion and non-violence, as a strength of civilization."

"He was copying Albert!"

"Dear Louise, I don' t mean to nitpick but let me remind you that *Promise at Dawn* came out in 1960, whereas your son wrote *Belle du Seigneur* in 1968."

"They were both machos, you know. They denigrated women at the same time they put them on a pedestal. They loved them and seduced them again and again. They couldn't live without women. But they only chose who adored them and showed them off. And these women had to hide their own intelligence, shrewdness and above all their critical powers. Romain and Albert were too fragile for any of that."

"I was just wondering why we always sought out the company of men," said Louise. "We've been here for years and none of us misses them at all."

"Speak for yourself!"

Minnie Marx had just entered the garden, wearing a loose black dress.

"To think I have to come outside if I want to join in this conversation, when you know how much I hate gardens. I only feel good with my feet on the asphalt, breathing in the smells of the big city. I love the company of men, their freedom and spontaneity when they go after a woman, and I love in particular that they don't sit around analyzing everything all the time."

"In that case, don't let us keep you," Mina shot at her, insulted.

"No, I like you all too much. Can't I admit that men amuse me? My husband especially."

"That's because you took him for one of your sons."

"It's true he behaved just like them, which only made me love him more. He was a tailor, his clients sarcastically called him 'the ace of spades' because he didn't know his way around a needle and thread. He used to say that only amateurs used a tape measure; professionals like him could take a measurement just by looking. The results were lamentable. You could always pick out Samuel's clients by their too short sleeves and the uneven hemline on their trousers. Once was enough though; they never came back after that. Samuel wasn't bothered, though. He only had to go a little further from home to find new clients. He was an optimist above all else. He refused to worry and tried to make the most of every day. It was a wonderful philosophy for life and he passed it on to Harpo."

"Was he much involved in his sons' upbringing?" Rebecca asked.

"He helped the most by doing the cooking. When even I couldn't convince a theater director to book the boys, he could always win him over with one of his dishes. He could turn a few ingredients into a mouthwatering meal. But there were always too many of us and too little to eat."

"Did he realize that you loved your sons better than him?"

"Well, he could see who was the toast of Broadway and it wasn't him."

Minnie blinked a few times then suggested that they all go in.

"We'll be more comfortable inside, don't you think?"

Back in the living room, Minnie poured herself a glass of scotch and threw herself into the story of her life with her husband. The German neighborhood where they lived on New York's Upper East Side was teaming with immigrants just like them, looking for a better life in the city's bustling streets. Simon Marrix had come from Alsace, but once in America he decided he would be Samuel Marx.

"How did you meet?"

"You can't guess, can you, how a Frenchman ended up with a German woman? He had to cross the whole Atlantic to find himself surrounded by Germans!"

"Did you catch sight of each other on the boat that brought you to Ellis Island?"

"Not at all," sighed Minnie, nostalgic now. "I did arrive by boat, of course, but with my parents. I was sixteen years old, and it was 1880. We've all heard the stories about Ellis Island: the confusion, the dirt, the humiliation . . . I was mesmerized by the ship's wake. I thought it was tracing the line of my destiny in the water. I was young, strong and absolutely determined to succeed. I loved watching the sun dance on the waves so I told myself that, whenever I doubted myself, whatever might happen to me, I only had to see the sun sparkle, even in a puddle, and I'd get my courage back. It was a glorious day. I was so sure of myself. It was just a superstition of mine, but it proved useful. It helped me find Samuel, on a ferry one bright sunny day when the sea shone like all the constellations in the summer sky. It was the winter of 1882. I could hardly see my future husband's face under the wool cap he wore, but he got my attention. He helped me into the boat, and we were together from that day forward."

She was moved by the memory and reached for her handkerchief.

"Is everyone here an exile?" Rebecca asked.

"There's Jeanne Proust, who never left Paris, and Amalia Freud, who stayed in Vienna. But the rest of us all know what it's like to live at the whim of politics."

4

Exile

Thinking about Minnie's arrival in New York, Rebecca started to draw a mental picture of what life would have been like for the Cohen's and the Kacew's. Albert came to Marseille in 1900 and Romain Gary to Nice in 1928. Greek and Russian, respectively, both were from poor Jewish families who had left their native countries behind. Theirs was a world that no longer existed, and they had known the horrors of the 20th century. Both mothers had only their sons, to whom they were devoted, and the sons had only their mothers. And Rebecca? She hadn't experienced any tragedies in her life. The fall of the Berlin Wall? She had watched it on television. War, massacres? She'd seen pictures in newspapers. And yet, she had protected Nathan much like these other women had protected their sons, with the same undying hope that they had put in their sons' futures. If they had made something of themselves, if they had proven themselves to be exceptional, it was because these women had breathed so much energy into them.

Is some kind of trauma a precondition of future success?

Rebecca was curled up in a large leather armchair, leafing though a photo album with Mina. She lingered over a portrait of Romain Gary when he must have been no more than fifteen years old; he had a thoughtful look, fine features and wore his hair combed back. He was remarkably handsome and elegant, with his tie carefully knotted around the collar of his starched shirt.

"Even when he was little, Romain was as serious as any adult," Mina remarked.

Smiling to herself, she got up to find a shoebox in a cupboard, then returned to her spot next to Rebecca and began to shuffle through more photos until she came to one in particular. It was Romain again, this time buckled into a leather jacket, an aviator's cap down low over his forehead, a sly smile under his thin mustache, hands in his pockets and a swaggering look in his eyes.

"This was taken when he joined General de Gaulle. After that he was made a Compagnon de la Libération and became French, too," Mina declared proudly.

Rebecca fished around in the box as well. It was full of Kacew family photos.

"When did you leave Russia?" she asked.

"Right after the fall of the tzar, in March, 1917. We weren't the only ones to leave, you can imagine. People were in a panic. We were lucky to find a spot in a cattle car."

Mina's voice never wavered as she talked about this most dangerous moment of her life. She might have been talking about moving from one house to another in the same street. She was strong, sure of herself and of her rights.

"I never had a thought for anything other than Romain's well being. So many things could have gone wrong. I made him wear camphor around his neck to keep away Typhoid fever but, above all, I never took my eyes off him. He was incontestably the most beautiful person in the whole car, and I convinced myself that, with eyes like his, he would make it out of there."

"It's true he had beautiful eyes."

"You think so, too! Deep and blue, intelligent and sad at the same time. Romain knew how to melt you with just one look. Seeing him reassured me through that whole exhausting trip across the European continent in flames."

"Where did you get off?"

"At Wilno, where the train stopped. I had intended to go all the way to France so Romain could grow up and study and become someone, but it was impossible to go any farther."

"Are Wilno and Vilnius the same city?"

"Oh yes, just like Vilne and Vilna. The city has four names, which gives you an idea of its complicated history."

Mina explained that she was so traumatized by this uprooting that she found herself hating History itself. Human relations, love, friendship: these became the only things she cared to think about. Political theory bored her stiff. But it was difficult to ignore what was happening all around her; politics defined the age in which she lived. Nevertheless, she allowed herself to go into some detail with Rebecca.

"Lithuania was part of the Russian Empire until its independence in 1918, before it was invaded by Poland in 1920. With Jews making up almost forty percent of the population, Vilnius was *the* capital of Yiddish intellectual life. They came from Poland mostly, a few from Belarus and there were Lithuanians, of course. It was one of the busiest cultural centers in the Jewish world. It lived up to its reputation as the Jerusalem of the North. We could have stayed but I was obsessed by France."

"How long did you live there?"

"Five years," she answered curtly.

"It must be difficult to talk about your life there," Rebecca acknowledged. "I'm sorry if my curiosity has seemed indiscreet."

"Not at all. It's just that I've almost forgotten our life in Wilno and Warsaw, wherever we were before we arrived in France: I was so determined to get there. Even back then, I could pass for being French and I was raising my Romouchka to be both a diplomat and a French writer. I taught him Russian, Polish and German, Jewish stories and Lithuanian folktales, but above all I taught him French history. There was a book that I read to him again and again: *Lives of Famous French People*: Louis Pasteur, Joan of Arc, Roland at the Battle of Roncevaux. I wanted Romain to be in that book, too. I was full of hope and affection for the man he would become. I would tell him over and over that he had the soul of a hero. I believed in him."

Rebecca looked at Mina's souvenir box: It was full of photographs of Romain. For her part, she didn't like taking pictures; the innumerable questions of light, perspective and distance got in the way of seeing, and then the instant was gone. She wondered now, though, if photos didn't in fact help you remember. Without them, would the faces of loved ones fade? Would the details of life dissolve? No, Nathan's features would remain forever engraved on her memory: the chubby-cheeked baby who had become a skinny little boy before transforming into a handsome young man. She could remember clearly every moment of his life. But what would Nathan remember of her? Would her expressions gradually vanish from his memory, until only a halo remained? Do we ever truly see anyone, even the people we love? Her gaze paused on a picture of a young Mina: a green-eyed, pale-skinned, high-cheeked brunette. She was wearing a white dress, a string of pearls and her hair was caught back by a headband. She was stretched out in a field, smiling and relaxed, holding a cigarette.

"I smoked to beat the band," Mina remembered. "Even after I got old. I thought that having a cigarette in my hand made me look young and healthy but the truth is I was overworked and diabetic."

Rebecca was fascinated. Where did this little Russian woman find such willpower? Alone and penniless, how did she manage to get herself to France when all of Europe was heading for war? Why did she have such faith in her son's future?

"That's just how it was. I always knew. And so did Romain. France was where he would make a name for himself. And that's what happened. Didn't he say himself that there were only two people who had the best interests of the country in mind: me and General de Gaulle? When De Gaulle rallied his countrymen to join the French Free Forces in 1940, Romain didn't hesitate, but it was my own urging he responded to as much as the General's."

Louise Cohen burst in, looking like a Greek shepherdess in a long skirt of rough cloth and carrying a tray of fruit juice.

"You're talking so much, Mina, I thought you must be thirsty."

"Do I detect a note of irony?" Mina asked.

"No, but you're telling Rebecca a lot of nonsense, whereas I think she ought to have a clear idea of what things were really like at the time."

Rebecca steadied herself for Mina's inevitable outburst, but, unexpectedly, she only sighed.

"I suppose you know everything that happened to me even better than I do," she said to Louise. "It's one thing to live through important events; knowing how to tell a story about them is another."

While Mina poured herself a glass of juice, Louise took Rebecca aside.

"What Mina has forgotten to mention is that Wilno was a living hell for her. She was boasting of the intellectual life there, but the Jewish quarter was filthy and its narrow streets were canals of stagnant sewer water. She lived in a building called 'Le Petit Versailles' but she barely earned enough to pay the rent. Eventually, she had to leave, like so many others, but Warsaw was no nicer. What with the famine and Pilsudski's dictatorship, it became impossible to live in Poland."

Mina, who had heard everything, suddenly piped up:

"What did we care? We were headed for France in any case."

"If Warsaw had been welcoming and comfortable, you never would have left and Romain wouldn't have become Romain Gary, World War II Hero. He would have stayed Roman Kacew. Your son's destiny was to collide with history: you had no choice but to leave."

"Think whatever you want," replied Mina. "It's all the same to me."

"Don't get so angry," Louise retorted. "Go ahead and fool yourself that it had always been your decision to emigrate to France, that you had always planned to stop over in Vilnius and Warsaw. You can embellish the past all you want."

"But it's the truth, Miss Know-It-All!"

"Do you really think you can just rewrite history like that?" Louise insisted.

Trying to create a diversion, Rebecca interjected: "How did you get a visa to enter France?"

"You could always get a fake visa," Louise answered before Mina could say a word. "But in that case it was best to enter through Italy."

"So, you did have a fake?" Rebecca asked Mina.

"That's none of your business. All I'll say is that the police captain who processed our papers was adorable. I told him that I had been forced to come to the Mediterranean climate for my health and he told me where the best places were to go. He had fallen under Romain's spell."

She stood up with the air of an actress delivering the last lines of a tragedy.

Never able to let anyone else have the last word, Louise Cohen also got to her feet and turned to face Mina.

"The France you entered in 1928 was not as wonderful as you'd have us believe. How could you live in Marseille, or in Nice for that matter, with no money and no relations? You might have had two years of French at school and been a passionate francophile, but it's impossible that you could have felt at home."

Mina turned as pale as if Louise had slapped her across the face. Rebecca didn't like the way the conversation was going. She took Mina by the arm and sat her back down, inquiring politely how they found things in Nice when they arrived.

"You have to understand that this pretty little southern city was like paradise to us. We had come from the gates of Hell," Mina explained. "We had already been uprooted when we arrived in Poland, even though we were staying with my brother and his family. You can't imagine how they treated my beautiful Romouchka. Like some common child! They had no idea what greatness was in store for him and I couldn't take it anymore."

"You sold jewelry and silver door-to-door, even daring to knock at the finest homes in Nice, pretending that your goods came from the Russian Imperial family, but you never would have made ends meet without your brother's help," Louise reminded her.

"He was horrible to us. However, we had a neighbor in our building who believed in Romain. He was only eight at the time but this neighbor was impressed by my predictions about his future. He would insist that Romain describe for him the immortal glory that awaited him and he would feed him Turkish delight. Mr. Piekielny was his name. He looked like some forgotten clerk out of Kafka. He used to ask Romain to say his name to the important people he would meet when he becomes famous. He was preparing him for his future. He believed in him while my own family made fun of my dreams of glory. I just refused to be a poor immigrant. My son was going to be an ambassador and a writer, and that would change everything for us."

"I would never have dared to dictate Albert's future like you did to Romain."

Mina seemed not to hear Louise, continuing her story unperturbed.

"We slept for a time in the waiting room of a dentist friend of ours. We had to be out every morning, but anything was better than my family's mockery. The dentist was a marvelous man who treated Romain like a prince."

"And you like a princess."

Mina blushed slightly at the mention of this trivial flirtation.

"Oh, I have to admit, he was charming and he seemed attracted to me. It lasted three months, until his nurse put a stop to it. She either had enough of us encroaching on her waiting room or she was jealous. She clearly had a thing for Gabriel. His name was Gabriel," she said with a far off look that betrayed some affection for his memory.

"She forced you out?"

"The dentist's wife complained to the nurse that her husband was coming home later and later and asked her to stop making evening appointments for him. She thought there was something going on between the two of them. So, to prove her innocence, the nurse told her about us, implying it was our fault he was so busy. He threw us out the next day."

"But your life must have been easier in Nice than in Warsaw?" Rebecca prodded.

"We were happy because we were together. I was content just knowing that everything I did was for Romain's good and that he had a proper childhood. I held every job imaginable: cleaning lady, dog groomer, saleslady at the Negresco Hotel. Finally, I became the manager of the Mermonts Hotel. That was luck! It was a Ukrainian whom I'd helped to buy a building who hired me."

"Is that so?" Louise scoffed.

"That's quite enough!" Mina burst out, truly angry this time, and with that, she was gone.

Louise Cohen now turned to Rebecca and pulled out a photo taken at the time of her arrival in Marseille: she was young and a little plump and was wearing a summer dress and a straw hat with a bunch of cherries on the brim. She and her son were walking and he was holding her skirt. It was hard to know who was protecting whom. Was it Louise, the Jewish mother, or was it little Albert, who, at five years old, was already careful to hide his fears from his mother so as not to worry her?

"It was difficult for Albert to adjust to Marseille, and for me as well," she began. "We felt quite alone in this France we hardly knew. Albert was my brave little man, wide-eyed, trying hard not to cry. But the big city was overwhelming for him, the noise of passersby, the speed of the cars. Marseille gave us a fright after our little island."

Jeanne Proust had come in solemnly, looking like a grand noblewoman, sat down next to Louise, and Mina followed. Had she gone to find an ally?

Jeanne interrupted, addressing Louise Cohen:

"You were an Italian in Corfu, you were used to being a foreigner by the time you came to France. I spent my whole life in Paris but I can imagine how hard it must be to feel at home in a strange country."

"There's no comparison! We were Italians in Corfu, it's true, but four centuries of Venetian rule left their mark. We felt at home there. In France, however, we were utterly lost."

"Now you've hit the nail on the head!" Mina joined in. "I was already French in my soul before I arrived there. You on the other hand, didn't even know who you were or where you came from. I don't know why, Louise, you insist on believing we endured the same hardships. Our experiences weren't alike in the least."

Rebecca looked from one to the other. Mina was heavily made-up and her short hair was carefully combed around her face. More discreet and natural, Louise emanated a certain grandmotherliness. Physically, they were opposites, but their personalities were strikingly similar: determined, domineering, inflexible and hypocritical. Two peas in a pod!

Louise Cohen was unstoppable now on the subject of her exile.

"I wanted Albert to be French but it was just as important to me that he understood where he came from. So I did what I could: I put him in Catholic school in the hope he'd rub elbows with the French elite and at home, I told him stories of the Jewish royal houses and all their customs and ancestral traditions. I would never have allowed him to become one hundred percent French; it would have created a gulf between us. On the other hand, nothing delighted me more than to read about the adventures of the Valiant family. They were eager, imaginative and sincere, as all of us are who call Corfu home."

"I suppose the Valiants' grand arrival in Geneva took place with a bit more pomp and circumstance than yours in Marseille?" Rebecca wondered.

The allusion made Louise laugh; how could anyone compare her to Albert's daring and resourceful characters? She was not too shy to admit, however, that she admired his novels' portrayal of the immigrant's fear of rejection. He had written from experience.

"No matter how much Albert thought of himself as stateless, each move was an uprooting for him," Louise continued. "He grew to like every city: Marseille, Paris, Geneva, London, Jerusalem, and he wanted to become a French citizen, but wherever he went, he always said the same thing: 'My home is somewhere else.'"

"Perhaps he felt he was Jewish above all?"

"He could hardly have forgotten that fact. We left Corfu as so many Jews did, just as a tide of anti-Semitism started to grow. This was in 1900. A young Jewish girl, Rubina Sarda, had been found murdered just before

Passover. Suspicion immediately fell on the Jewish community, including the girl's father. People thought it had been a ritual sacrifice and some arrests were made. But this gave rise to more generalized violence, insults and attacks against Jewish businesses. The family was acquitted but the damage had been done and the atmosphere was suffocating, even though Corfu had been admirably tolerant to Jews up until then. Jews had even obtained equal rights from the French in 1791. If we were persecuted, we remained united, and resigned. In Marseille, however, things were far worse."

"How so?"

"For one thing, we arrived just after the Dreyfus Affair."

Jeanne Proust interrupted curtly. She had no interest in hearing tell of the unfortunate captain; it brought up so many unhappy memories for her. Her Adrien had been stubbornly pro-military and anti-Dreyfusard and their differing opinions on the scandal had provoked disintegration of their marriage. In fact, they had had a bonafide argument about it that only cemented their lack of understanding. After that, she had always felt that she was living with a stranger.

"That may be," Louise Cohen replied dryly. "But you had the good fortune to live in Paris, such a cosmopolitan city, not like us in Marseille. We had hardly gotten settled in our hotel room when we were robbed of everything."

Tears welled in her eyes at the memory.

"I got over it, but Albert became more and more withdrawn. He avoided boys his age and seemed different from them. He had such a fine imagination, I thought he would adjust, but the humiliation he endured on his tenth birthday was the final straw. We were out, and he was dressed in his sailor suit: such an innocent soul! He stopped to watch a street peddler selling a sort of stain remover. The peddler was a smooth operator, and Albert was fascinated. I remember him smiling, looking at the crowd that had gathered. He had found a good spot in the audience from which to observe the man's performance and for a moment he felt as if he belonged among these French people, whom we had idealized so much. Emboldened by that thought, probably, he decided to buy three sticks of the stain remover and held the birthday money I had given him out to the man. But the peddler yelled right in his face: 'You? You're nothing but a kike, a dirty Jew; I can see it on your face. Ladies and gentlemen, allow me to present to you one of Dreyfus' pals, come to steal the food out of the mouths of the French.' Well, I won't repeat any more of his anti-Semitic slurs. They were common coin back then. That was the end of Albert's childhood, though. He lost all his joy from one day to the next. That happened on August 16, 1905, and he wrote many years later that that was the day his life became his destiny. The episode comes up many times in his work. I knew nothing of his feelings at the time, however. Albert didn't share anything with me; he was too sensitive to burden me with his sufferings."

Jeanne Proust was deep in *The Guermantes Way*. She was looking for the passage where Bloch wonders if Norpois, the ever prudent diplomat, was a Dreyfusard or not. She knew the page by heart. Her expression brightened when she found it, and then she began to chuckle indulgently as she read the Duc de Guermantes' reply: 'When one goes by the name of "Marquis de Saint-Loup," one isn't a Dreyfusard; what more can I say?' She never tired of rereading the literature of the great Marcel Proust, her son! She was still bristling from Louise Cohen's snub and, holding a book in her hand, allowed her to follow the conversation without having to say a word.

"Why must Louise Cohen always bring the conversation back to anti-Semitism?" Mina was asking Rebecca. "Was Albert particularly bothered by it? He must have had a depressive nature. My Romain, on the other hand, was the most carefree child, despite all we endured. All the pogroms in Poland alone! I can give you figures . . ."

Louise interrupted her: "Do you really believe that Romain was happy?"

"I've never been surer of anything in my life. If you want to carry the worries of the world on your shoulders, go right ahead. It all depends on how you look at things."

"I don't know why I bother to talk to you, Mina. You think you're the only person who has ever known what it's like to work hard for something. And evidently, you've never felt the slightest doubt, either. I can't say the same. I was never sure my son would be successful, and I sometimes felt powerless to fight off life's unexpected turns. I forced myself to be a good little soldier, though: I did what I had to so that Albert would have a better life than mine, and I tried to give him what he didn't have. But I knew I couldn't work miracles, either."

"You're right," Mina conceded. "The difference between you and me is that I always believed in miracles, in large part because I could never tolerate complainers, whiners or cry-babies. God gives us a life; it's up to us to make something of it. It took a lot of work to hide our difficulties from Romain so he wouldn't have to worry. I wanted him to have a better life, just like you, Louise, and he did. Things weren't always rosy at the Mermonts, but we had a roof over our heads and our clients often became our friends. And however bad things were, I always made him believe that ours was the most wonderful life. We were different and we were proud of it: we were Russians in Nice, Jews in Russia, atheists among Jews. We had no allegiances, belonged to no clan; we lived for each other, by ourselves, on the outside. We weren't unlucky. It was just the way we wanted to live."

Mina's words had a humbling effect on Louise Cohen. She drew her hand across her forehead, patted her chignon in place and sank a bit more deeply into her armchair.

"I was mistaken, perhaps. Maybe you really were happy."

"I think Romain was," Mina replied with a victorious smile.

She began to animatedly paint a scene of their domestic bliss: picnics of rustic bread and Malossol pickles at the beach and how she would hold her son close to her in those tranquil moments at the seaside that filled her with happiness.

Louise excused herself:

"It's natural to judge from one's own experiences, so it seemed to me our situations were similar. But I was thinking about Albert, as usual, not about myself," she added wearily.

Rebecca was worried again for Nathan. Like Louise, she couldn't get her mind off her son, and she was sure he was grieving for her. There's no shame in showing one's pain, but eventually that has to end. She was afraid he would tire his best friend, even though Arthur would certainly have tried to shake him out of his depression and get him back in the swing of his daily activities. What was Nathan doing now? What was Nathan doing now? Had he returned to his classes at the university? Or was he home alone, grief-stricken and shut off from the world? What if he couldn't get over her death? Her son seemed to have none of the emotional strength of Romain Gary or Albert Cohen, who had weathered so many storms. Nathan had never had the time or the occasion to become famous; why was Rebecca in this place anyway?

5

Playing Favorites

*A man who has been his mother's
indisputable favorite never loses that feeling
of a conqueror, that confidence of success that
often induces real success.*

Sigmund Freud

Amalia Freud was seated at her damask-draped dressing table, applying red polish to her nails. Rebecca was watching her, uncomfortable with her sudden proximity to this *grande dame*, whose authoritativeness intimidated her but whose opinions seemed invaluable. Perched erectly like a schoolgirl on a chair in the corner of the bathroom, she observed her surroundings, from the clawfoot bathtub in the middle of the room to the gilt mirror hanging above matching sinks.

"You never talk about your daughters," Rebecca said. "Didn't you have five girls?"

"Daughters are the future mothers of boys; it would be wrong to treat them as children. As soon as they are able, they must learn to help their mother and at times fill in for them."

"You asked your daughters to help with the housework, but never your sons?"

"What's wrong with that? My golden Sigi was a special breed of human being. Is that why he was my favorite, or did he become a genius because I was more attentive to him? I can't say. No one contested his preeminence in the family, however. His sisters owed him their respect and obedience."

Reaching into a cupboard, Amalia pulled out an oil portrait of Sigmund with his sisters. He must have been twelve at the time. In the picture, Anna, the eldest daughter, was holding a garland of roses, Mitzi, a basket of flowers, Rosa, a delicate branch, and the two others, Dolfi and Paula, were standing on either side of the youngest child, Alexander, who was holding a whip and a puppet. Sigmund had a book in his hand.

"A picture is worth a thousand words," Amalia remarked. "And Sigi was aware of his importance, even if he wrote to Alexander once that they were like book covers containing the story of their weaker sisters. He knew he was the head of the family."

"And that he was your favorite?"

"Of course; it was obvious. Besides, he had the largest bedroom to himself."

"You mean, his sisters were crowded together somewhere else in the house?" Rebecca asked, unwilling to believe that such a blatant injustice could be dealt in such an offhand manner.

"Exactly. They shared a single room. Nothing was more important than Sigi's comfort; he needed absolute calm to be able to work. When I learned that he was upset by his sisters practicing the same pieces of music over and over at the piano, I didn't waste a minute in getting rid of that infernal machine. Moreover, when he became a father, he forbade his own children to play an instrument. He said it was because he hated music, but I think it was because he was always wary of exposing his emotions. Silence was safer."

"That's a psychological explanation. I thought he just didn't have an ear for music."

"How could he have been able to read peoples' souls if he knew nothing about music?"

Her tone of voice was unequivocal; it was clear that Amalia would entertain no more discussion of the matter. Her attention had turned to her image in the mirror as she powdered her already pale face. The two women remained silent.

"What if one of your daughters had shown talent for the piano?"

"I don't see what you're driving at, Rebecca. None of them could hold a candle to Sigi; he was a brilliant student. I realized, when he was only five years old and I was teaching him to read, that he was very quick to understand and was curious about everything. At that point, his father took over the responsibility of his lessons. He was always the top student in his class at school and he scored brilliantly on his Matura at the end of secondary school."

Amalia ran her fingers through her long braid to undo it and began brushing her hair.

"That's not how things are done anymore."

"No more teacher's pets?" Amalia interrupted, leaving Rebecca no time to explain her point.

"I mean that spoiling children is a taboo subject. People prefer not to discuss it."

"Then you're a generation of hypocrites."

"Sigmund was the prince of the family, and no one was jealous?"

"Yes, Anna, who was born just after him. She was outraged that he forbade her to read Balzac and Dumas. She used to hide in the linen closet with her books."

"And you did nothing to stop the little tyrant? You could have taken Anna's side and told Sigmund that he had no right to dictate to his sisters."

"He had a natural and indisputable aura of authority. I never questioned it because he was right about most things. I pampered him and made a fuss over him; he was so fragile, my golden Sigi!"

"More so than his sisters?"

"His brother, Julius, was the exception. He was born just after Sigmund also, but he died of an intestinal infection."

"Oh! I'm so sorry," Rebecca cried. "I had no idea."

"You can't know everything."

"How did Sigmund handle it, when you told him that Julius was dead?"

"We never spoke of it."

"I had forgotten that before Freud, no one explained anything to children," Rebecca remarked.

"That has nothing to do with it. From one day to the next, Julius was suddenly gone. What more can I say? He was only 18 months old. How could I ever have guessed that he might have wanted to get rid of his younger brother so he could have all my attention to himself? I never suspected how much his death affected Sigmund. It was only later that I learned he felt that he'd killed him. All his ideas about sibling rivalry and the Oedipus Complex stem from that experience."

"Sigmund never acted differently?"

"My own brother had just died of tuberculosis. The two deaths became rolled into one. I had named my baby after my brother; it brought him bad luck. I should have been more careful."

"You couldn't have predicted any such thing. Julius was probably a fashionable name in your day. Groucho Marx was named Julius, too."

"I was exhausted, physically and emotionally, and I was alone. I couldn't count on Jacob; he spent half the year away from home, selling his merchandise in Spain, Hungary, Germany and Austria, and my brothers lived far away too. I never saw Sigi's distress and I never forgave myself for it."

"But then, how do you explain the idealized vision he kept of his early childhood, before you moved to Vienna? I remember he wrote in one of his letters that 'the happy child' that he had been in Freiberg 'continued to live' in him. Why would he have remained so attached to that city?" Rebecca asked.

"My son was a genius, but there were things about him even I didn't understand. What could he love so much about a village of five thousand people surrounded by flat, grey plains? Everyone seemed alike, whether they were merchants or shopkeepers or brokers or door-to-door salesmen, and they all spoke Yiddish. The textile trade was flourishing, and Moravia was a prosperous region, but it was a miserable, provincial life we had there compared to Vienna."

"Maybe he liked the house you lived in?"

"It was a fairly large house we had, at 117 Schossergasse, but it wasn't very comfortable."

Amalia pulled a photo from her pocket and showed it to Rebecca. The house looked as if a child had meticulously drawn it, with two floors and two large windows and a square, stone roof. The owner's name, J. Zajic, could be seen clearly on the facade.

"Freud never liked Vienna, but he couldn't leave it either."

"I thought he fled to London, in 1938, a year before his death?"

"That was thanks to Marie Bonaparte, one of his wealthy patients, who exerted all her energy and influence on him to leave. Even the war and the painful cancer in his jaw couldn't make him leave. I'm still angry at him for his stubbornness: if he had left earlier, he could have saved his sisters. Or tried to at least. Four of them died in concentration camps. Luckily, Anna, the eldest, was in New York already, and Alexander was in Canada."

"Where were you living?"

"I died in 1930, before any of that. Sigi never understood the danger. When Martha, his wife, mentioned his sisters, it was already too late."

"Had they remained close?"

"Only he and Rosa, who was his favorite. Between his books and his patients, he had time for little else."

"And yet you still defend him?"

Rebecca was convinced that, if he hadn't been taught to put his own interests before everyone else's, he could have helped his sisters leave Vienna when he did. She didn't dare say this, but Amalia guessed her thoughts and stood up.

"Rebecca, you had just one son. You can't understand. Sigi was my golden boy and he still is. He needed constant attention, which is why he managed to surround himself with three mother figures. Did you ever think of that?"

She explained the family structure: Jacob had had two sons with his first wife, Sally. He then married Rebecca, who never bore him any children, and this second marriage remained a mystery to Amalia; Jacob never spoke of it and she didn't even know if his second wife had left him or had died. Perhaps she had committed suicide. Amalia never found out. Neither could she have imagined, when she married Jacob, that she would become the head of the family for his two grown sons, who were as old as she was. But it seemed natural that Emmanuel, his wife, Maria, and their children should have lunch with them every day. She loved John, their son, and so did Sigi: The two boys were inseparable.

"Maria was like another mother for Sigi, as was Monica, his governess. He wore out those who loved him the most," Amalia remembered. "I was amazed to learn that at the end of his life, he had surrounded himself with another trio of surrogate mothers: His wife, Martha, his sister-in-law, Minna, and his daughter, Anna."

"Did you prefer him over your other children because of a rivalry with the other two women? Because you wanted to be his favorite among the three? Or was he just the oldest child who gets all the attention?"

"I don't know," Amalia shrugged. Rebecca's questioning had tired her. "Ask Jeanne: she neglected Robert and devoted herself to Marcel."

Amalia and Rebecca had been walking for some time, passing from one room to another.

"Should we look in the library?" Rebecca suggested.

"How can she continue to read Proust all the time?" Amalia wondered in return.

"Maybe she reads to learn more about him," Rebecca offered. "Marcel Proust is still a subject of many books."

"As is Sigi, but I'm not as zealous as Jeanne. When I read what psychoanalysts have written about him, I feel like it's a foreign language."

Jeanne was indeed deep in an obscure treatise on her son when Amalia and Rebecca opened the large doors of the library. She put the book down regretfully.

Amalia didn't waste a moment telling her what they had come for: "Rebecca wants to know why Marcel was your favorite son."

Rebecca began to cough, embarrassed by Amalia's directness. It had not been her intention to question Jeanne's judgment, and even less to be manipulated by Amalia.

"Yes, I paid far more attention to Marcel than to Robert," she began, settling herself into a chair with the contented look of a mother who has been asked to talk about her children. "But I didn't favor him over his brother. Robert was two years younger than Marcel and he learned immediately to take care of himself. I had an easier pregnancy the second time and I think that this had something to do with his development. He never needed me. Confident and strong, he took after his father, whereas Marcel almost died at birth. Their lives were like their childhoods. Robert followed in Adrien's footsteps and became a famous surgeon. He was the first to ever perform an ablation of the prostate, and he successfully achieved the first open-heart surgery, in 1910. Marcel, on the other hand, depended on me to support him his whole life."

"You mean to say that your second son was a genius too?"

"Yes, but no one would know much about Robert if not for Marcel."

"Wasn't he jealous?"

"As soon as he was old enough, he made it a point to protect Marcel," Jeanne explained. "He knew his older brother was different: more sensitive and delicate, more complicated than he was. So he understood instinctively that I couldn't raise the two of them the same way, and he never took it the wrong way."

"I seem to remember, though, something Georges Duhamel wrote about how much alike they were," Rebecca countered. "Duhamel was a surgeon as well as a writer and he noticed, watching Robert operate, that he had the same slowness, the same languor as Marcel. Also that they shared an almost obsessive faith in good breeding and an uncommon ability to listen to people."

"He's entitled to his own opinion," Jeanne retorted.

"But isn't there a photo of Marcel and Robert, looking perfectly elegant in their grey suits and smart little boots, where Marcel has his arm around Robert's shoulders in a protective gesture, looking just like a concerned older brother?"

"They were still young then. I think they switched roles in the end. Robert, my other wolf, eventually became the older brother, quite naturally."

"You didn't actually call him that, did you?" Rebecca asked, surprised by the term of endearment.

"Marcel was 'my wolf' and Robert was 'my other wolf,'" Jeanne admitted with a peal of laughter.

Robert de Saint-Loup's name was no coincidence then: a fusion of both the brother's name and the mother's nickname for her sons (from the French 'loup'). Brilliant and cultivated, elegant, terribly handsome, impertinent and individualistic, Robert de Saint-Loup cuts a dashing figure as the best friend of the Narrator of *Remembrance of Things Past*, and dies a war hero at the novel's end. He is also an introvert who keeps a mistress although he loves his wife. Could he have been modeled on Marcel's brother?

"Ridiculous," Jeanne declared, losing her temper. "How could he have thought of Robert when he created that character? Marcel liked to have fun with names, that's all. But you will have noticed, surely, that there are no brothers in any of Marcel's novels. He thought of himself as an only child, because that's the way I raised him, I suppose."

Jeanne Proust was speaking now of Marcel's notebook from 1908. In it, he relates the end of his summer holidays that year: Marcel was to stay in Illiers while his mother and Robert were to return to Paris. He was beside himself at the idea of being separated from his mother. Robert, on the other hand, was furious that he had to leave the baby goat he had adopted, and ran off, hoping to delay their departure. Jeanne caught up with him as he was setting off down the railroad tracks. Terrified, she tried to pull him off but he grabbed hold of the tracks. Adrien arrived and slapped the disobedient child. Jeanne, meanwhile, was explaining the situation to Marcel, who understood everything already: his father was upset that she was leaving and if Marcel made a scene about her leaving, too, Adrien would be out of patience with both mother and son. Proust was conscious of the inseparable couple that he formed with his mother; he was nothing at all like his rebellious and immature younger brother.

"Robert must have suspected my feelings for Marcel," Jeanne admitted. "At lunchtime, he would complain that Marcel was served more chocolate cake, which is the worst sort of injustice to the mind of a hungry boy with a sweet-tooth. But Marcel didn't just want more cake than his brother; he wanted all the dessert for himself."

"He wanted to be loved by his mother, more than anyone else; brother, father or anyone."

"He knew he was," Jeanne said, overcome by emotion.

"And what did Robert think?"

"Robert's wedding will give you some idea of what our family was like," Jeanne began. "The day got off to a bad start: both Marcel and I were ill. It was a nightmare. Like at any wedding, there were two families, but not like you would expect to see. In our case, the only interesting people to watch were the Weils and the Prousts. Why would I have even pretended to care about Robert's new in-laws, since it was obvious I would never again lay eyes on the Dubois-Amiots? There was Adrien, bursting with pride to see such a handsome and self-assured son of his marrying so well, thanks to himself; Marthe was the daughter of one of his mistresses. It marked a great step up the social ladder, and you could hardly get in the door of Saint Augustine's Church with all the fashionable people and their elegant hats. With that marriage, Adrien was leaving Illiers, that small town of his childhood, and his parents' shop where they made wax, chocolate and honey, far behind him, forever. He was thrilled with himself. And then there was me, sickened to death and wounded by this wedding that Adrien and his mistress had concocted. I had had nothing to do with any of it. I managed to be welcoming to his relations and his colleagues from the hospital, but as soon as the ceremony was over, I let it be known that I was too tired to go to the reception hosted by the Dubois-Amiots. No one tried to change my mind; I hadn't been at the civil ceremony either. I'd been laid up by my rheumatism, but don't suppose I'd done it on purpose; I was miserable."

Marcel arrived late. He was wearing a heavy coat layered over another, with a thick scarf around his neck even though it was July. He looked terrible. All the attention paid to his brother had made him feverish; either that or he wanted to show solidarity with his mother. The wedding took place, and it proved that Robert was more a Proust than a Weil.

"I didn't like my daughter-in-law, Marthe, because she detested Marcel," Jeanne remembered. "They never fought but her intrusion into our family was enough to set off all kinds of conflicts. Fortunately,

Robert never listened to what she had to say and always came to visit Marcel face to face. But he couldn't stop her from throwing out any letter from Marcel that she happened to find."

"How do you know that if you were already dead by then?"

"I read it. You know, you can learn a lot here, especially about famous people. What Marthe didn't realize is that she could have made a tidy sum selling his personal correspondence. Instead, she burned most of it, because she thought everything he wrote was indecent, dubious and shocking. She thought his very existence was shameful."

Rebecca considered the possibility that Robert's wife was jealous of Jeanne's feelings for Marcel. Perhaps Marthe thought that her hatred of the favorite son would be a comfort to her husband, who had been excluded from a similar relationship with his mother.

"I wonder why you read George Sand to Marcel and not Robert at bedtime. I heard somewhere that you skipped over the more troubling pages of *The Country Waif*. Why did you choose a novel about incest for a bedtime read?"

One passage still stood out in Rebecca's mind. In it, a peasant boy, a bit of a simpleton, is about to be sent to an orphanage by his mother, but he faints and catches the attention of Madeleine, the miller's wife. She takes pity on him, embracing and kissing him, and offers to raise him herself. She becomes a kindhearted mother to him, but he falls in love with her as he gets older. Why would Jeanne choose to tell the story of their incestuous relationship to her son, especially one as fragile as Marcel?

"The novel describes a surge of tenderness," Jeanne protested. "I also read him *The Devil's Pool*. George Sand was one of my favorite authors."

"Apparently, he only remembered *The Country Waif*; he references it in *Remembrance of Things Past*. It must have troubled him if he was still thinking about it years later."

"Oh! You find bad intentions in everything!" Jeanne burst out angrily, just as she did every time someone found her at fault.

"Did Minnie Marx have a favorite son?" Rebecca wondered out loud in an attempt to distract Jeanne.

"Her favorite was Chico, her eldest," Jeanne replied matter-of-factly.

Leonard was his given name but Chico was the stout one of the trio who spoke very fast with an Italian accent and played the piano with a "revolver hand" as if he were shooting the keys.

"Shall we go find his mother?" Jeanne proposed. "Minnie avoids going out and hates the library. That's just the way she is."

They spied her ample form and waves of blond hair in the sitting room. She was perched at the piano, singing a music hall number. They waited until she had finished.

"Rebecca would like to know why Chico was your favorite son," Jeanne declared.

"Why are you all so tactless?" Rebecca exclaimed angrily. "I've had enough of your rudeness!"

Minnie merely smiled. Like Jeanne, she was delighted by the chance to discuss her life with a newcomer.

"Chico was the oldest," she began, looking at Rebecca. "I adored him right from the start and I never stopped. He wasn't more talented than the others; quite the contrary. He was a compulsive gambler: horses, craps, roulette, poker, bezique, you name it. He had competition at home; my husband and I were both experienced players. But Chico took it to an extreme. He could gamble away ten thousand dollars in a single day. His brothers didn't let him get into much trouble. They agreed to invest what they made on *A Night in Casablanca* rather than let him throw it away at a poker table. He was able to live comfortably from those earnings for the rest of his life. Journalists would ask him: 'Chico, how much have you lost gambling?' And he'd answer: 'Ask Harpo how much money he's saved. That's how much I've lost.' Even when he was little, he would pawn anything he could find, and the house was in such chaos we didn't notice right away if something was missing. Once we did, we knew where to find it; there was constant traffic between our apartment and the money-lenders."

"That didn't bother you?"

"Chico was funny, and I knew his happy-go-lucky personality would be his saving grace. He used to say, on the days he lost at gambling, that he knew he'd win again, and on the days when he won, that he was sure he'd lose again. He always managed. His talent for accents was a survival skill in New York City, you know; he could do Irish, German, Italian . . . He amazed me as a little boy. He was always wonderful, but not in the same way when he got older. "

Jeanne Proust couldn't help putting her two cents in:

"You must be referring to Marcel's theory that a person is a series of different and sometimes contradictory selves."

"If it pleases you to think so, be my guest," Minnie replied.

Every mention that Jeanne made of Marcel put Minnie on edge.

"Say whatever you like, but my sons were funnier than Marcel, including Zeppo, who wasn't even a professional comedian."

"You didn't know Marcel like I did. You don't understand his sense of humor, but I do. Whenever I'm bored, I think about the scene in *Sodom and Gomorrah* where the Duc de Guermantes learns, on his way to a party, that his cousin Amanien d'Osmond has died. 'He's dead! That can't be! You're exaggerating!' he exclaims. Well, I always chuckle at that scene, like so many others from *Remembrance of Things Past*."

Minnie leaned towards Rebecca and whispered:

"If Marcel had been my son, he wouldn't have been so la-di-da."

"You would have made him into a gambler, is that what you mean?" Jeanne asked drily. She had heard every word.

Four of Minnie's five sons had been the toast of Broadway. It was her brother, Al Shean, who had become famous on the vaudeville circuit, and convinced her that they had a career ahead of them.

"I always thought Groucho was the oldest."

"He was the most famous of them all," Minnie conceded. "But God knows he drove me crazy. He hated gambling, and the rest of the family teased him for his puritanical attitude. Worse, he was serious, with intellectual airs and a misanthropic streak. My third son was completely different. The first two—Leonard, whom you know as Chico, and Adolph, who was Harpo—were handsome and blond. Then Julius was born; he looked like a horribly wrinkled prune with black hair all over the place. Just the sight of him was enough to set you off. Odder yet, he was born angry."

"Groucho wrote: 'My mother loved children; she would have given anything if I had been one,'" Rebecca cited from memory.

"I do love children but I always treated mine as if they were adults," Minnie corrected her. "Why must we glorify and idealize childhood? My own was dreadful. Being a young child is oppressive, physically and mentally. You have to be home on time, you can't go out without telling an adult, and you have to do what everyone expects of you. Challenging an order or questioning a decision is inconceivable. At home or at school, you have to be like everyone else. It's suffocating. So I never treated my children like they were children."

"Do you think Groucho felt unloved?"

"He certainly tried everything in his power to make me like him, poor thing. You'd think he had a sixth sense for knowing what would please me. He could read my moods better than anyone and he was always on the lookout for ways to sweet-talk me. But it never worked. I mistreated Groucho as much as I idolized Chico, who could not have cared less. I had a soft spot for Harpo too, but not in the same way. He was closer to my husband than to me."

"Harpo, who plays the harp rather than speak. Was he actually dumb?"

"No, but he was touchy. A theater critic once wrote that his high-pitched voice undermined his acts, although he was naturally funny and had an undeniable presence on stage. That was it, though: he vowed to never again speak in public. It only made him funnier."

"Perhaps it was you who convinced him."

"I don't think so. I can't remember anymore."

Jeanne Proust's mood had turned morose, and when she was like that, she had a habit of twisting a lock of hair around her finger.

"It's not Groucho who suffered the most in your family," she put in.

Minnie bristled at the remark. She was perfectly capable of putting the blame on herself but she refused to be accused by others.

"If you want me to admit that I sent Gummo off to fight in World War I in Chico's place, I won't deny it. I chose him to go because he was the least talented of his brothers for comedy and could add nothing to their act."

Rebecca's horror must have shown on her face because Minnie excused herself.

"I did everything I could so my boys wouldn't be called up. I bought a farm outside Chicago because farmers were excused from the draft, but it didn't help; Gummo had to go be a hero. I know I was unfair, but he came out of it just fine, and when he returned, he had the perfect pretext for turning his back on the stage, which he hated. Instead, he became an excellent promoter and manager of his brothers."

"You always find a way to be right," Jeanne remarked.

"Precisely. And everyone knew it. Family meant everything to me, and I was the one in charge. The boys were successful because they were so closely knit. They were 'The Marx Brothers' above all, even if each of them had his own identity: Chico the Italian, Zeppo the ladies' man, Harpo the silent clown. Groucho was the most famous, as you know, but only because his career spanned more than seventy years. He was a star of music hall and Broadway, movies, radio and television. He wrote seven books, including the hilarious *Memoirs of a Mangy Lover*, a play, two screenplays and almost one hundred articles . . . Still, he wouldn't have come to much without his brothers. Even when he wrote alone, he used them for material. I'll give you an example of something he said to justify his refusal to write a humor column: 'How can anyone do this every day? What is there important enough in the world to fill up this much white space every 24 hours? Why don't they just leave it blank and say Harpo wrote it?'"

Minnie burst out laughing. She was feeling jovial now. Touching up her red lipstick, she proposed a game of musical chairs. Jeanne Proust and Amalia Freud thought it a splendid idea. Rebecca, on the other hand, detested the game; since there is always one chair less than there are players, someone is always the odd one out. She hesitated. Alive, she would never have accepted, as she was always the loser. However, if such rational and intelligent women as Amalia and Jeanne insisted so much, she could hardly refuse. Minnie gave a new rendition of the vaudeville tune she was singing when they came in. They all laughed like little kids. Dumbfounded, Rebecca watched them run and push each other and throw themselves on the chairs with so much conviction that she forgot to play. She was the only one standing as the older women in their long black dresses guffawed at her.

6

Rebecca

*I've made mistakes in my life. For one thing,
I was born. That was my first mistake.*
                                    Woody Allen

*I refuse to join any club that would have me
as a member.*

                                    Groucho Marx

Rebecca wanted to be alone to think about these women whom she was beginning to know intimately. Louise Cohen seemed the most honest to her; she put her son on a pedestal like the others but she could still harbor doubts about how she had raised him. Mina fascinated her; she would forever be in love with her Romain, who was some kind of rare perfection. Still, she found her too competitive to ever become a true friend. Minnie Marx treated her like a domineering mother, the same way she treated everyone else. Amalia Freud intimidated her. And she was careful about Jeanne Proust, too well behaved to be totally honest.

She ventured further than she had before, but there was nothing to be found: only the blue, cloudless sky and silence. A total emptiness beckoned the mind to let go of all preoccupations. Everything that Rebecca had been, everything that had made up her being, now seemed far away to her. She let herself float . . . It was heavenly. She wondered if this was the ultimate high that drug addicts seek, to be outside oneself in a thick and restful, cottony cloud. When she was alive, she had been a control freak; she could never have let herself go like she was doing now.

It occurred to her that if she wandered further she might get lost. Would she forget Nathan? Was that even possible? Wasn't her son the one thing that she loved? If she had shown interest in her students or if certain books had enchanted her, only her son truly kept her invested in life. She had had no friends. Caught up in her courses and research and conferences, brooding endlessly over her son, Rebecca had never taken any time for herself. She had some girlfriends from her university days, of course, and they could spend hours discussing the placement of a comma in Flaubert. He had a famous line: 'For me, the most beautiful girl in the world is nothing next to a perfectly placed comma.' An opinion Rebecca shared; for her, nothing was better than a well-written book! The few childhood friends who had remained close were like a fine wine to her: their flavors and intensity had changed with time but on occasion still left delicious notes she was happy to find again. New friends weren't part of her baggage, though. She had Nathan.

But he wasn't with her in this place. She regretted terribly that she could never ask his forgiveness. She used to nag him constantly about his manners, his taste, his degree of culture. She realized now that maybe she had been wrong. Nevertheless, she hadn't the slightest idea how to raise a child by complimenting him and respecting his opinions and decisions. In the end, she had been a terrible mother; rather than make him jump through hoops to become a lawyer, she should have indulged him a little and encouraged him to find himself. If he was unhappy, if he lacked self-confidence and was unable to convince anyone of his worth, including himself, it was her fault. Nathan's pessimism reminded her of something Woody Allen says in *Annie Hall*, when his character is telling his therapist the story of two elderly women at a resort in the Catskills. One woman says: "Boy, the food at this place is really terrible." The other one says, "I know, and such small portions." Woody Allen's character concludes: "Well, that's essentially how I feel about life—full of loneliness, misery, suffering, and unhappiness, and it's all over much too quickly."

How badly had she failed Nathan? She had paid both too much attention to him and too little. Whenever she would ask him what he was doing, she only half-listened to his answer, for fear she wouldn't be able to resist imposing a contradictory opinion. She never wanted to be a dictator. Too often, she had lost her temper and had made him feel her own worries, but she had fawned upon him too. Maybe he would turn out alright? All these mothers had raised their children in their own way. What had they done better than she?

Rebecca imagined the joyful disorder of the Marx household where creativity was king. She couldn't remember ever making Nathan laugh. He usually regarded her with apprehension, as if he expected a critical remark, as if he could never please her. But their lives had certainly been more peaceful than the Cohens', where Albert's instinctively violent father had been "the male and the tamer" who had reigned in terror over his wife and son. Albert felt sorry for his mother, whom he considered a victim. That had never been Rebecca's problem. Then there was Mina; her suffocating, vampiric love had undoubtedly ruined Romain's life: no one could ever love him as she did. He admitted it himself: "In your mother's love, life makes you a promise at the dawn of life that it will never keep." With the Prousts, on the other hand, the trick was to be a good boy, or suffer the wrath of Jeanne's insidious harassment. She fooled herself that her abusive attention to Marcel was "for his own good." She would tell the servants to turn down the heat in the evening in the sitting room so that Marcel couldn't entertain his friends, and she insisted he invite her to every dinner party he organized, so she could see who his friends were. He had no freedom whatsoever.

These thoughts left her confused. On the one hand, it seemed that she had nothing to be jealous of: these mothers' relationships with their sons were clearly flawed. On the other hand, she admired the fact that they had all done what they had set out to do; raise their boys to be successful men. Her mind returned to Nathan. It might seem that her indecisiveness had tripped him up. She was never sure if she was being too hard or too soft on him. But it was too early to say what might happen. After all, he was only eighteen. None of the famous sons of these women were celebrities at his age.

She began to imagine a glorious future for him. The dream didn't last, however. She was dead and buried: She could do nothing more for him. All that was left now was to trust in his abilities. No matter what opinions she might hold about these Jewish mothers, she knew they had never backed down from their mission, and their sons had made them proud.

Rebecca returned to the library. She wanted to read some of Romain Gary and Albert Cohen for herself, both about their mothers. *Promise at Dawn* is the story of Gary's childhood and adolescence, from his earliest years in Vilnius until his mother's death. He describes how Mina's overflowing love and ambition for him carried him to heights he never could have dreamt of for himself. *Book of My Mother* uses a more recitative style to tell the moving story of a woman who was as naive as she was self-sacrificing. Although Cohen remembers every moment he spent with her, he is remorseful at the idea that he never lived up to her love for him.

Rebecca was reminded of the waves of emotions she had felt as a teenager when she read Romain Gary's book. She must have been in high school because she pictured herself in her father's country house, where there was never anything to do during the long days of her summer vacation, except read. Since then, she had never known such boredom. She had briefly attempted to take an interest in her bucolic surroundings, in the hope of finding a new distraction, but the mere sound of the wind in the trees put her to sleep. A nature program on television had an even more soporific effect on her. She learned to keep to her room to avoid both insect bites and the smells of the cows, horses and pigs, and sought refuge in books, reading with a kind of bulimic hunger as if she too suffered from a shameful disorder that sapped her confidence and enjoyment in life. The long immobile hours, no matter how she positioned herself on a chair, the floor or her bed, made her legs stiffen with cramps, however, and a new wave of ennui awaited at the end of each novel. Sometimes she amused herself by looking for the word "boredom" in whatever she was reading at the moment. The exercise left her even more lethargic, if possible. She had picked up *Promise at Dawn* as a lighter read, in between *Finnegan's Wake* and *Moby Dick*. It hit her like a lightning bolt: such understanding, complicity and love between a mother and her son seemed extraordinary to her. It marked her as deeply as *Book of My Mother*, which she had read in high school and found even more moving for not having a mother herself.

Feverish now, Rebecca was anxious to find the others. She felt alone and isolated, far from everything. She went looking for them but found herself wandering for a long time in endless space.

7

Success Shall Be Yours, My Son

> *Guynemer! You will be a second*
> *Guynemer! Your mother has always been*
> *right ... An Ambassador of France, a*
> *Chevalier of the Legion of Honor ... a new*
> *Gabriele d'Annunzio.*
>
> Romain Gary

> *A mother finds true satisfaction only in her*
> *relationship with her son, on whom she can*
> *transfer her own suppressed ambitions.*
>
> Sigmund Freud

"Rebecca?"

Hearing her name called from the dining room, she went in to find Amalia Freud spreading jam on slices of bread.

"Would you like a cup of tea?" she asked, looking up with a smile.

"I'd love one," Rebecca replied, relieved that Amalia looked happy to see her. The two women made quite a contrast: one sporting faded jeans and a loose pullover sweater, the other in a tight-fitting dress with her long hair in a neat braid.

"You seem preoccupied."

"How can I be sure my son will succeed in life?" she blurted out. "There's no magic formula and yet all of you managed it."

"Have faith," Amalia replied. "In my case, it was obvious Sigmund had a promising career before him. An old peasant woman had even predicted it; I can still remember her exact words when she saw him. 'With your first-born, you've brought a great man into the world.'"

"Maybe she was just trying to be nice."

"Possibly, but her words filled me with confidence, so that, later, when he was deciding between law and medicine, I could tell him truthfully that I would support him no matter what he chose. Jacob wanted him to take over the business. I thought he should make up his own mind. He proved me right by creating a profession that had never existed before: psychoanalysis. Sigi surpassed even my wildest dreams."

Amalia adjusted her shawl, which had slipped down over her bare arms. Then, with a coquettish toss of her head, she stood up and made her way towards a long table lavishly laden with breads, fruit and cereals.

"But, Nathan, what will become of him? No one predicted a great future for him."

"You worry far too much."

"He used to reproach me for only wanting to talk about his grades, but I couldn't help myself. I was a professor, so for me being a good student was as natural as washing yourself. He hated me for it, though. I was too demanding. But he was so intelligent. I thought his laziness was inexcusable, an affront to anyone who had a difficult time studying."

"Children find it hard to express themselves. That was his way of rebelling against you, without saying it in so many words. Maybe he wanted you to see he was his own person?"

"Oh, he knew ways of doing that! He invented an imaginary friend named Christian; don't ask me why. We had to set a place for him at the table and he talked to him constantly. Thinking he was lonely, I began inviting his friends over every weekend. But he never played with them. 'What's so interesting about a soccer ball?' he would ask me. All ballgames were the same to him; it was only the size of the ball that changed. He was bored by it all so he kept to himself."

"He had a wonderful imagination, no doubt. Instead of worrying yourself and criticizing him for being antisocial, you ought to have encouraged him."

"Is there anything left to eat?" Mina demanded, looking over the buffet. "Where is the coffee?"

"On the table, where it always is," Amalia replied. Mina was always in a terrible mood before she'd had her three cups of coffee in the morning. Amalia didn't hesitate to share this confidence with Rebecca in a low whisper. "The bad habits of an overworked woman," she concluded.

Mina poured herself a cup, grumbling under her breath, but Amalia had returned to her conversation with Rebecca.

"Why did you think Nathan ought to become a lawyer? A strong imagination doesn't lend itself to practicing law . . ."

"'Law opens the door to everything.' Or so the saying goes. And when Nathan told me he wanted to be a lawyer, I didn't realize that he was only trying to please me. He understood how impatient I was to see him on a clear professional path . . . as if he could choose a profession the way you choose which sweater you're going to wear in the morning. I wanted to direct him. I should have allowed him more time to think it over."

"Did you do everything you could to convince him?" Mina wanted to know, setting her coffee cup down. "Did you explain to him how famous he would be as a great criminal lawyer? Did you buy him a properly tailored suit? Did you make him feel the elation of seeing a client acquitted? Did you read him the speeches of the great defense lawyers? If he were my son, he would have been assured of his success before he'd ever begun. I would have painted his glorious future for him while he was still in his crib . . ."

"Did he know what he wanted to be when he was a child?" Amalia interrupted.

"Yes," Rebecca answered, embarrassed. "He wanted to become a pilot."

"Romain was a hero, as you know of course," Mina bragged. "His plane was shot down by German artillery. The pilot was blinded. Romain was wounded in the stomach and half-unconscious but he took control of the plane and managed to land it. He was decorated for his bravery, but I was no longer around to see it. I took credit for it though."

"How in the world did you do that?"

"We had dreamed so much of the distinguished life he would lead, that he eventually believed it. I know it sounded strange when he was little. Even the fruit and vegetable sellers in the market in Nice had to listen to my stories about what a great man he was going to be, but they came to respect me in the end."

Amalia leaned in a second time toward Rebecca: Mina was surely the only mother in the world who could determine her child's future. To help him bear up under the hardship of their daily life, all her bedtime stories began with "Someday you will be . . ." and continued with a list of everything he would accomplish.

"It worked like a charm," Mina agreed.

Seeing Rebecca's doubtful look, she added:

"I assure you, it's true. I already told you about that Mr. Piekielny . . . He would look with awe at Romain as if he had already reached the summit of glory. I'm sure he was just like me, Mr. Piekielny; he believed in miracles. Here was this poor little Jewish boy in France with a mother who was going to make him become someone, and so he had to succeed, just because she believed in him. I think the sheer force of my conviction kept Mr. Piekielny going for a while longer. He wanted to believe in the dream like I did. Romain worked tirelessly to prove me right."

"Do you really think he told the Queen of England that 'Mr. Piekielny lived at number sixteen, rue Grande-Pohulanka, in Wilno,' like he wrote in his novel?"

"He certainly did," Mina replied. "But this lovely man never knew it. He had already died in a gas chamber."

"Such a sinister conversation at the breakfast hour!" Minnie Marx exclaimed, bursting suddenly into the room.

"Don't sit down," Amalia warned her.

"And why not?"

"We're not spending the day here."

"And why not?" a laughing Minnie wanted to know again.

She turned to Rebecca and began addressing her as if there was no one else in the room.

"You did the right thing, choosing your son's profession. There's no telling what children might come up with on their own."

"I completely agree with you," Mina seconded. "Rebecca was not firm enough with the boy."

"All I wanted was for him to be happy," Rebecca explained.

"You see? You cared more about his happiness than his career."

"Obviously."

"It's not as easy as it seems. When you're young and idealistic, you can let yourself be carried away by the dream of a job that doesn't pay, and then regret it later. Being successful professionally is always one less thing to worry about. And it's something to make you proud, even happy, if that matters. I had such difficulty finding something that Romain was good at. We tried everything. I shouted to the rooftops that my son would be a prize-winning jockey, but he had no talent at all for it. It was the same with fencing and pistol shooting, which was a shame: I could just see him in the dress uniform of the Republican Guard! I taught him Latin, German, and French, of course, the Fox-Trot, the Shimmy . . . There was nothing I didn't try. Every failure was like a stab in the heart, but my greatest disappointment came with music: A disaster! His teacher finally told me, as sweetly as possible, that I was throwing my money out the window on violin lessons for him. My theory is that he couldn't stand the screeches. As if my son was the first mediocre pupil he ever had. He didn't get it. I would have paid him double if he could only teach my Romouchka to play well! But there was nothing to be done: I had to let it go."

Rebecca was mentally tallying everything at which Nathan had failed: music, fencing, soccer, chess . . . Images began to haunt her, like when she used to wake up at 5 a.m., seized by a panic attack. How did these mothers do it? How did they make their sons so famous? Was it enough to just decide they would be? Mina never gave up until she found the one thing Romain was good at and then, when he began writing, she still wasn't satisfied: he had to be an ambassador, too.

"What drove you like that?" she asked Mina. "Were you a fan of Claudel? He was a writer, a diplomat and a member of the Académie Française."

"Oh, he did get into the Académie after all?"

"In 1946."

"I was dead already. No, it was Chateaubriand I found the most exciting."

Mina, like the actress she had once been, declared:

"He lived through eighty years of French history and politics, traveled around the world, and he still managed to find time to reflect and to write. He even said this: 'I would like to have never been born or be forgotten forever.' I so wished my son would have lived that maxim. What good is it to live if not to become famous?"

"Such pressure!"

"Yes, but I knew Romain could do it, and he didn't let me down."

Minnie Marx, who until now had been absorbed by her eggs and sausages, turned to Rebecca while continuing to chew:

"It's better to make decisions for your children. There's always a job you would cringe to see them do."

Mina interrupted her:

"I was afraid Romain would want to become a painter. His teacher announced to me with great pride that he had talent, but I made him swear to never say so to Romain. As soon as he would start to draw, I would take away his brushes and pens."

"Why did you pay for lessons in that case?"

"Certainly not with the idea that he would mistake an elegant hobby for a profession. All painters end up penniless and mad."

Mina was categorical: A life of misery was the fate of every artist. She wanted her son to be famous and feted in his own lifetime. So she encouraged him to be a writer, and whatever he wrote she thought it was marvelous.

Minnie asked Rebecca if her greatest fear was that her son would become a pilot.

"I thought it was an unwise choice for someone so easily distracted. But what would have made me the angriest, would be if he had chosen to become a sociologist."

"What do you have against sociology?"

Rebecca didn't know, but she had always thought it to be a pedantic and meaningless way to earn a living.

"Was there a particular sociologist you didn't care for?" Minnie offered.

"Did you know many?" Mina wanted to know.

"No, I didn't. It was just one of those preconceived notions."

This line of questioning exasperated Rebecca. She had singled out that one profession on a whim, but the other women wanted to treat her comment as a serious opinion and debate its pros and cons!

"My greatest fear was that one of my boys would act in porn films," Minnie said.

"Did you have a reason for thinking they might?"

"Not at all; why do you ask? Groucho wanted to become a doctor."

"And you wouldn't let him?" Rebecca asked with a barely stifled cry of anger.

"Of course not. Why should he waste years studying when the theater was beckoning?"

"You must be the only Jewish mother in the world who stopped a son of hers from becoming a doctor! Do you know the one about the mother whose son is invited to a party?"

"No," Mina and Minnie responded in unison.

"She has two sons, five and seven years old. So she asks: 'Which one is the invitation for? The doctor or the lawyer?'"

"What's so funny about that?" Minna asked. "Doctors have the worst job in the world: they have to spend their days listening to people complain about their aches and pains and the never-ending litany of ailments of hypochondriacs. But actors just have to walk around in a tuxedo and a top hat to earn enough money to throw fist-fuls of it at the urchins in the street, like my brother Al did."

"Was it your brother who suggested your sons go into show business?"

"I had to force the hand of destiny," Mina recalled, stretching. "They were going to pot . . . Chico was gambling in a dive on 99th Street. Harpo had just said goodbye to his career as a bellboy. Groucho was acting part-time, and Gummo was still trying to convince his teacher that Paris was the capital of Greenland. The best way to be in the spotlight was to get hired together. I cooked up a little number and named us 'The Three Nightinglales.' Everything changed from that day."

"What did your children say? They agreed to that?"

Minnie looked squarely at Rebecca, flabbergasted:

"Did I give them a choice? I knew exactly what I was doing. I became their impresario, as I've already mentioned. Harpo tried to put up a fight, protesting that he couldn't sing. I told him to keep his mouth open and pretend. No one was the wiser."

Rebecca imagined a plump, young Minnie besieging every theater agent in town, negotiating contracts and accompanying her new act from city to city before settling in Chicago, second only to New York for vaudeville. She didn't hesitate to rename herself Minnie Palmer, thinking it was sexier and better for business. Nothing could stop her.

"When I found out that the smaller vaudeville troupes were paid by the number of members in the company, I persuaded my sister Hannah to perform with us, so we could be paid three hundred dollars instead of two hundred."

"What if none of you had been talented? I suppose that wouldn't have bothered you?" Mina asked with a touch of malice.

"Certainly not."

At forty-four and forty-two the sisters dressed up as schoolgirls and took off their glasses. When they sat on the same chair, it collapsed under their weight. And that was the end of their show business debut.

"We had to rename ourselves 'The Four Nightingales.'"

Rebecca was thrilled by Minnie's energy and confidence.

"How did the Marx brothers get their start? Beyond the name, which might have been a problem, did you envisage specific roles for your sons?"

"Except for Harpo, they all had nice singing voices until they reached puberty, and then I had to develop their act," Minnie remembered, as if it was still 1918 and she was looking for ideas. "Groucho pretended he was a German actor, and Chico debuted his famous Italian accent, which he had copied from his barber. He only had to imitate him and people burst into laughter. It amused him, so he continued the act in the theaters and then in film."

"Did you write the shows?"

Minnie sighed. Was she offended? There was no way of knowing, since she abruptly left her plate half-finished and began pacing up and down the room, breathing like a bull.

"Yes," she said.

Coming from a chatterbox like Minnie, it was a short "yes." Rebecca couldn't resist the temptation to ask again, prompting her to finally admit that the only time she had been absent from the troupe, they had had their biggest success ever.

"They were in Ann Arbor, Michigan," she began. "I had told them to end with a song. 'If they whistle at you as you're leaving the stage, you're done,' I told them. But they didn't agree with me; they wanted to end on a comic note. We left it there because I had to go find a tenor: ours had flown the coop, but his operetta solo was the highlight of the act. 'School-days,' it was called. Worse, he had left with the only tuxedo we owned. It's true that it did belong to him . . . Groucho decided to take matters into his own hands by proposing to sing Verdi's hit, *La Donna è Mobile*. I told them, 'That's all well and good, but what about the tuxedo?' I was serious; it gave the act a touch of class. Chico found the solution: he told me to fire the pianist and, with the money saved, to rent a tux. I thought it was all settled when I left.

"Groucho kicked off the act as the tenor but suddenly stopped. 'I don't like your key, Giuseppe,' Chico told him, then sang the same piece in A minor. 'That's worse!' Groucho yelled at him. That's all they needed to raise havoc: Harpo ran back on stage, threw Chico off his stool and started playing. Since he didn't miss a beat, Groucho kept singing *La Donna è Mobile*, in Italian.

"That's when they went crazy: Chico on the piano stool, Harpo on his shoulders and Groucho who could just reach the keys by wrapping his arms around Chico from behind, and singing all the while. Eventually, they all fell over. They were called back seven times for a bow. For the first time, the Marx Brothers were in all the papers."

"What was your reaction?"

"Well, I never found a tenor, so I came back empty-handed. Then when I read the review, it was like a punch in the chest, all the more so because they did their number in the second act, which was supposed to be the musical half of the show. By nature I'm pretty stubborn and I never admit I'm wrong. I began whistling *La Donna è Mobile* to myself, wondering what I could possibly say to them. Then I found it: 'You know, I always told you that comedy was our forte,' I said."

She laughed heartily.

"They would never have amounted to anything without me. Never."

Jeanne Proust came in, looking surprised. "I wasn't expecting to find you still here. I finished eating hours ago."

"Today, Minnie isn't going anywhere," Mina remarked dryly.

That was good news to Jeanne Proust. She could eat breakfast all day if it was to talk about her Marcel! She knew she had a sympathetic listener in Rebecca.

"Did you let Marcel decide what he wanted to do with his life?" Rebecca asked her.

"Do you remember what Madame Santeuil says to her son? She tells him he's free to choose as long as he becomes a judge, a lawyer or a diplomat."

"That's fiction," Rebecca reminded her. "What about you? Did you worry about that kind of thing too?"

"Adrien wanted Marcel to have a serious occupation so he found him work at the Mazarine Library. I was the one who made it possible for Marcel to dedicate himself to writing, and I convinced Adrien that our son should no longer waste his time in an unpaid, meaningless position. He needed regular hours but not an office."

"You got him started by forcing him to translate Ruskin."

"He didn't have a gift for English so I translated it and he rewrote it in good French."

"I don't mean to question the scope of your influence," Rebecca began. "But don't you think he would have become a writer anyway, with or without you?"

Jeanne threw Rebecca a look of pure hatred. If she could have made her disappear, she would not have hesitated. She began to shake, her chignon came undone and she turned red in the face.

"I did everything in my power to help him, to wrest him out of his intellectual stupor. I watched over him, I taught him how to apply himself, to be disciplined. Write on his own? You must be joking!"

Rebecca had finally had enough of these conceited mothers who considered themselves indispensable to their children's success. She shouted back at Jeanne:

"But he waited for you to die so he could write *Remembrance of Things Past!*"

Jeanne jumped, her inflamed cheeks now pale. She took a moment to calm herself. Mina patted her forehead with a damp napkin, while Minnie poured her a glass of water. Amalia, who had come back in time to witness the scene, suggested she needed something stronger and handed her a glass of straight scotch.

"No, it's too early for that," Jeanne Proust managed to murmur. She never lost her good manners.

"Oh, go ahead," Minnie encouraged her.

Jeanne took a sip, sighed deeply and turned to Rebecca:

"The discipline and routine I imposed on Marcel are what allowed him to write *Pleasures and Days* and *Jean Santeuil*. We woke at the same time, we ate our meals together, and that's how he was able to write his masterpiece."

"It seems to me that didn't really work," Rebecca insisted. "He soon returned to his old habits of working at night and sleeping during the day, living in his bed."

"Just like Minnie, I had to finally acknowledge that I could do nothing more for him. The main thing was that he continued to work hard."

"But if you had seen the superhuman effort he put into writing thousands of pages, you would have stopped him from killing himself at it."

"That may be true," Jeanne admitted. "Nothing is harder on a mother than to see her son suffer."

"He managed fine after your death. I doubt he would have been able to write so candidly if you had continued to be his principal reader."

"If you're referring to his homosexuality, he knew that I knew, without saying it in so many words, of course."

The other mothers were surprised to hear Jeanne Proust speak so openly about Marcel's private life. This haughty woman had never before even alluded to the subject. They looked at each other for an uncomfortable moment, then Minnie broke the tension with a question for Rebecca:

"In the end, what was it that your Nathan was good at?"

"Reading," Rebecca said in a low voice.

They all began to laugh, with the exception of Rebecca, whose embarrassment they didn't even notice.

"Didn't you say you were a French literature professor?"

"Yes, precisely. That's probably why I never glorified reading. When that's all you do, you cut yourself off from other people's preoccupations and lives. You become a misanthrope. Excessive reading is an obstacle to accomplishing anything."

Jeanne Proust immediately burst out:

"But that's ridiculous!"

She had struggled so hard to instill a love of literature in Marcel.

"How can you be cultivated without reading?" she wanted to know, as if it was the only thing that mattered.

"What's so important about being cultivated? If it's to be boring, it's not worth it, unless you enjoy it, of course."

"But, you didn't prevent your son from reading, did you?"

Jeanne, who had received a much more solid education than most young women of her day, knew what an intellectual life was worth, and now she was almost purple with indignation. When she was young, girls were trained only in hygiene, cooking, cleaning, and deep breathing to help tolerate the pain of tightly laced corsets and narrow shoes. Jeanne was something of a phenomenon in her time, having learned Latin, English, German and the Classics from her mother. Af first, knowledge had pleased her, then it became vital to her happiness.

Louise had returned and, for the first time, they were all assembled in one room: Amalia Freud, Mina Kacew, Minnie Marx, Jeanne Proust and now Louise Cohen, too. What had brought them all here? The desire to see their sons become successful. Louise, however, did not share that view.

"Mothers aren't the only explanation," she countered. "We do what we can to help them in life but, in the end, they are who they are. In fact, I wonder why we were all killing ourselves for. Love and success are two different things. Albert was assigned to the diplomatic mission of the International Labor Organization in Geneva, and I can assure you that I had nothing to do with that."

Rebecca had to agree with Louise. In those moments when she had been proud of her son, she had not felt that she was personally responsible. So many other factors combine to make a successful individual: environment, biology, genes, energy, motivation and luck.

"It's possible that the Marx Brothers never would have existed," she argued, addressing herself to Minnie, "and Romain wouldn't have become Gary, but I doubt it. I think Albert Einstein still would have been a genius with or without his mother's help!"

Rebecca watched as a look of unease went around the room. They were observing each other, silent, in shock.

"What did I say?"

Minnie broke the uncomfortable silence.

"Without his mother, Albert Einstein would have wasted valuable time before becoming a physicist. He was three years old before he ever spoke a word. Mentally retarded or simply caught up in his emotional world? Who can say?"

Jeanne Proust explained that Pauline Einstein was so horrified by Albert's deformed head when he was born that she decided, then and there, he would have to be a genius. From that day forward, she was particularly tough on him.

"Albert didn't have anything specifically wrong with him," Jeanne continued. "But Pauline always made believe he was the top pupil in his class. Everyone knew, of course, that he didn't do very well at school. He said himself, later, that he 'wasn't a particularly good student or a particularly poor one.' His biggest trouble was with rote memorization, especially of texts."

Rebecca remembered a story about Einstein and his father, when he was about four or five years old. Albert had been ill, so his father gave him a compass. Einstein could still remember his astonishment, sixty years later when he told the story, when he first saw the compass' needle in its glass box. Sealed under glass, it was isolated and untouchable and yet it was irresistibly attracted by an invisible force that moved it to the north. It was a discovery that changed his life, or at least his conception of it. He was a genius!

"It's thanks to his mother that he turned out as well as he did," Minnie interrupted. "His father was against Albert embarking on a long course of study, just like me with my boys. He would have preferred to see him go into electrical engineering. But a mother's will always prevails, particularly when she's made an idea her hobby horse. Don't forget that Albert Einstein had a habit of repeating under his breath the same words he had just said. That would sound very strange indeed. Can you imagine?"

Minnie did an imitation of what Einstein would have sounded like, which provoked wild laughter all around. Satisfied that she could still win over a crowd, she stood up and adjusted her corset.

"It's unbelievable how much I love to laugh," she said. "Good thing for me I wasn't Albert Einstein's mother. It would have been a disaster, I'm sure; I can't vouch for his talents as an actor or even his sense of humor, even though his own mother assures us he was hilarious."

During this lengthy exchange about Albert Einstein, Rebecca wondered if his mother was somewhere and if she was going to suddenly appear in the flesh, so to speak. To prepare herself, she searched her memory for anything she knew about Einstein's parents. Nothing, except that they had made a fortune as grain merchants and had even been licensed to sell corn to the Württembergs: The royal family, no less.

"You're a walking encyclopedia!" Minnie marveled.

"Let's go to the library. I want to look up a few things," Rebecca said. To her surprise and pleasure, all five women followed her. She was one of them now!

To hide her emotion, she quickly looked up the entry for Pauline Einstein: 1858–1920.

"Just seven years difference between the two of us," Minnie Marx smiled.

"Both Germans too."

"We have a lot in common," she grumbled.

Rebecca paused, expecting Minnie to say more as she typically did when contradicted, but she was silent. Rebecca was impressed once more by Minnie's uncompromising character. She couldn't help asking:

"Won't Einstein's mother join us, or will she keep to herself like Woody Allen's? I still don't understand this place at all."

"Take my advice: Don't ask too many questions," Amalia replied.

"Shall we go somewhere where there's a little more light?" Minnie suggested.

Back in the living room, as Louise Cohen was discreetly leaving, Rebecca stretched out on a soft sofa since Minnie was starting to tell Einstein's life. "When Hermann and his brother Jack emigrated to Milan with their wives and children, they left Albert in Munich so he could finish his year at the *Gymnasium*. He was fifteen at the time. But when it became apparent that he was as hated by his classmates as he was by his professors, his mother sent for him to join them in Italy. This meant the end of his formal schooling, of course. However, his math teacher had written a letter attesting that he had a university level of knowledge and capabilities in math. So, after a year off, he took the exam to enter the *Polytechnicum* in Zurich to study civil engineering. He failed it . . .

"But he passed his physics and math exams brilliantly, leading the director of the university to personally counsel him to return to school in Aargau and earn his diploma there first," Jeanne interjected. "By then, he had already wondered what a light wave looks like. What fifteen year old asks himself such a question?"

"I'm guessing he passed the entrance exam the second time for the *Polytechnicum*," Rebecca wondered out loud.

"Yes, thanks to Pauline, who never stopped believing in his extraordinary potential," Minnie reminded everyone.

"Either that or he was born a natural genius," Rebecca replied.

Minnie Marx yawned. She had a quick wit and was easily bored, unlike Jeanne Proust and Amalia Freud, who never tired of talking about their sons.

"Shall we play a game?" Minnie asked.

"What kind?" Rebecca wanted to know.

"Let's play 'The Most Successful Son' because I have a feeling I'm going to win it today. After all, didn't the Marx Brothers bring out thirteen movies in twenty years, make a fortune and lose it all, while their fame never waned?"

"Who in the world gives you the right to declare yourself a winner? Where's the game in that case?" said an exasperated Mina.

"Go ahead then," Minnie challenged her, sounding like a referee in a boxing match. "Your turn!"

"Romain won the Goncourt book prize twice," Mina shot back. "The first for *The Roots of Heaven* in 1956 and the second for *The Life Before Us* in 1975. He would have easily been elected to the Académie Française, but he didn't put forward his candidacy."

"Yes, but he cheated!" Jeanne Proust exclaimed. "He published the second book under a pen name, Émile Ajar, because you can't win the Goncourt twice. Marcel won it by six votes, beating Roland Dorgelès by four votes. He was also decorated with the Legion of Honor in 1919."

"Marcel was incredibly talented, I'll give you that," Mina conceded, "But he was only a writer. My son, on the other hand, was a Companion of the Liberation before he began in the French diplomatic service, which sent him to Bulgaria, Switzerland, Bolivia and New York, where he worked for the United Nations from 1952 to 1954, and then Los Angeles, where he was the French Consul General from 1957 to 1961, when he finally retired from the Ministry of Foreign Affairs."

"Citing dates doesn't make him more important," Jeanne chided. "Romain Gary was an important man, and you certainly did well for yourselves but look where it got you!"

That was the final straw for Mina: Jeanne was wicked to have alluded to Romain's suicide. Pale and haggard, she was preparing to leave when Louise Cohen rushed in.

"Don't tell me I missed a round of 'The Most Successful Son'!"

"You're just in time," Jeanne said, patting a few loose hairs back into her chignon.

"The Marx Brothers were the most influential!" Minnie asserted, returning to the attack. "I only have to remind you of a few of Groucho's famous lines; they're common parlance now. For example: 'I must admit, I was born at an early age.' Or, 'Age is not a particularly interesting subject. Anyone can get old. All you have to do is live long enough.' Or, 'I worked myself up from nothing to a state of extreme poverty.' Remember this one? 'Why should I care about posterity? What has posterity ever done for me?' But my favorite is this one: 'Whatever it is, I'm against it.' I wonder actually if I didn't come up with that one myself."

"Is there anything he ever said that you disliked?"

"You mean do I love everything he ever said? Well, you won't hear me criticizing him. Go find Nettie if you want to hear a mother talk badly of her son."

"That's crazy! Woody Allen won four Oscars: two for *Annie Hall*, one for *Hannah and Her Sisters* and one for *Match Point*. And he was nominated eighteen other times! Not to mention the fact that he's averaged a film every year since 1970! What more does she need?"

"It's hard to believe he's never won our contest. No wonder Nettie angers so easily," Minnie declared.

"Yes, but whatever anyone says, Marcel Proust beats them all, even Albert," Louise Cohen insisted. "I'm not saying that to be nice to Jeanne either."

Jeanne was blushing with pleasure nevertheless.

"When Pauline Einstein used to lower herself to join us, she would win every time, hands down. Who can beat a Nobel Prize in Physics? And you can't deny that $E=mc^2$ is used to explain absolutely everything."

"It's even printed on t-shirts," Rebecca agreed.

"Did you know that it wasn't his famous Theory of Relativity that won him the Nobel but his Photoelectric Law?" Jeanne told everyone, sounding every bit like a teacher's pet who can't help herself from blurting out the right answer, even though she knows she'll be ridiculed later by her classmates.

"Why is that?" Rebecca asked.

"Because he hadn't finished working out his Theory, but his supporters were becoming more and more impatient. He'd been nominated every year from 1910 to 1922. Finally, the Nobel Committee had to find a way to give it to him."

Rebecca was amazed that these women still enjoyed having the same conversation. They must have played the game a thousand times because each of them knew by heart the minutest detail in the lives of these men and had apparently repeated over and over every variation without ever tiring of it.

"Louise, why do you want to let Proust win?" Minnie Marx wanted to know. "You never take my side . . . You don't play fair!"

"Fine, you win this time."

"But, why?" Jeanne burst out. "I don't agree. Didn't Proust write the longest novel ever?"

Mina was enraged:

"If it's weight that matters, Gary wrote thirty-two books: Almost ten thousand pages."

"That's an absurd criterion!" Louise Cohen countered. "Think about it: Albert wrote relatively little: eight books, some of which were versions of each other, since *The Book of the Dead* became *Book of My Mother* and *Belle du Seigneur* was written in 1938 and then rewritten in 1968. That said, it was a best-seller, translated into fifteen languages, even at 845 pages. It still tops the charts for Gallimard's 'White' collection. The number of bookshelves they can fill shouldn't be taken into consideration."

"Of course not," Minnie Marx said, upping the ante. "It's not the number of books that matters but the number of films!"

That was the final straw. They jumped to their feet, insulting each other, purple-faced and disheveled. For a moment, stunned by the turn of events, Rebecca had the impression she was watching a film with the sound off. She thought of Bonemine, the wife of the village chief in the Asterix comic books, who is always wielding a shield, a fish, a rolling pin or whatever she can find, to beat her opponents silly.

Deciding she ought to head things off before the women came to blows, Rebecca began to tell them the story of Astérix, whom they obviously had never heard of. They were soon mesmerized by the adventures of the tiny Gallic village that held out against the Roman Empire. However, when she explained to them that the story was a comic strip, they protested, disappointed, that "engraved literature" was of an inferior sort.

"What does this Bonemine look like?" Minnie asked in the hope of appearing interested.

"Small and pudgy but in a haughty way; she's proud to be the chief's wife. She's also domineering and knows how to get her way. She may be a housewife but underneath, she's a general."

"Just like me," Minnie observed.

"Does she have a son?" Mina interrupted.

"No, not that I remember, but I'm not an expert."

"So why do you even mention her?" Jeanne scoffed. "Go and find the mothers of Woody Allen and Albert Einstein since you want to meet them so much!"

Jeanne's remark was like a slap in the face to Rebecca. She lashed out, incensed:

"Why did you drive your sons so hard? For your own egos or your own pleasure? Romain is being completely honest when he writes in *Promise at Dawn*: 'I attached no importance whatsoever to my past or present; all that mattered was that I knew myself destined to reach those dizzying heights so clearly visible to my mother's eyes; nothing on earth could prevent me from reaching them for her sake. I had always known that my mission on earth was one of retribution; that I existed, as it were, only by proxy.' Retribution! That's what your sons were for you: pay-back! They only existed to avenge your miserable lives! They weren't autonomous beings; they were incapable of imagining their lives without you. At best, they were your clones."

Total silence fell over the room.

Feeling themselves under attack, they filed out of the room one after the other. Why did no one answer her? Was it because Nathan wasn't famous? But who could say that he wouldn't be, one day?

She returned to the library, chose a book, opened it at random and inhaled its odor of glue, dust and old paper. This smell always soothed her. Feeling better, she decided to find out what she could about the sons of her new companions; she really only knew them through their literature, but now that she had started to get better acquainted with them through their mothers, she wanted to form her own opinions. She started with Romain Gary, who had written in *Promise at Dawn* that he only existed by and for his mother, whose repressed artistic ambitions he had been groomed to fulfill: "I was determined to do all I could do to make her, by proxy . . . a famous and acclaimed artist." Gary had played the game. He wanted to prove to his mother that *her* life had not been in vain, that *she* had succeeded. He pushed aside his "me" in favor of an "us" that enclosed the two of them in a protective bubble. He adored his mother and was convinced he lived in osmosis with her. As he was leaving for England to join General de Gaulle's Free French Forces, he had an image of himself getting on the plane, but it wasn't him, rather "a fierce old lady, dressed in grey, stick in hand, and a Gauloise between her lips." It was his mother who was leaving, who had decided to fight and win the war, who was going to fly a plane. "I truly believe that it was my mother's voice which was talking through me." Who was he, then? Himself, his mother, or a combination of the two? He returns to the question later in the same book, when he finds himself walking in the medina in Meknes. He realizes that Mina has taken over his life as surely as if she had stolen from him and that there is no room left for himself.

Rebecca wondered if she had been reading out loud: an angry Mina had come running into the library to tear *Promise at Dawn* from her hands.

Taken aback, Rebecca let the worn paperback edition she had been reading fall to the ground, where it nearly broke into pieces, its spine ruined by hours of reading.

"Why did you do that?"

Mina mumbled an excuse, something about how she didn't need to read it anymore since she knew the text by heart.

Rebecca tried to please her and quoted a passage:

"Your son wrote this about you: 'Nothing could happen to me because I was her happy ending.'"

Mina smiled:

"It's true that my love for him saved his life. I had him paged as he was getting on a plane. I wanted to kiss him one last time. I'm sure my handsome Romain pretended to his friends that it was a lover who was calling him away. Delightful as ever, he missed his flight. But the plane he was supposed to be on crashed, leaving no survivors. My call saved his life."

"We're all narcissistic and egomaniacal," Rebecca observed.

Her remark lightened the mood.

Mina went on about her hero, all the while rearranging the curios that were piled on the fireplace mantel. The room was furnished to suit her: a bit too kitschy, loaded with colorful throw cushions, gaudy flowers and ornate furniture.

"He did better than I ever imagined he would. He wasn't content to come home a war hero, no! He managed to find time in the middle of a war to begin his first novel, *A European Education*. To think I wasn't there to congratulate him—I died in 1943 before the war ended—just makes me ill."

"I understand completely how terrible that is," remarked Jeanne, from a chair across the room where she had taken a seat. "I died before Marcel ever became famous, too. I hope you feel better after your little decorating spree but don't worry too much. Though I've done my best to teach you what good taste is, you'll never learn."

She was about to hold forth on the fine arts but Minnie interrupted her, crashing into the sitting room singing *I'll Say She Is* at the top of her lungs.

"Did I ever tell you about my boys' first Broadway hit? This was the hit song from their movie."

She arranged everyone in a line and, gesticulating as if she was an orchestra conductor, directed them to sing in unison. She was as full of life as she had ever been.

"Were you at the premiere?" Rebecca asked.

"You can't imagine how nervous I was," Minnie began. "It was the greatest moment of my life. I had dreamed so often of that day and then to think it had finally arrived! Performing on Broadway was a feat in and of itself, but that wasn't enough for me. I wanted to hear the public laugh, the critics applaud, bows and ovations—a triumph! I was in such a state of anticipation that, to ward off any disasters, I began reciting to my husband all the things that could go wrong. It drove him so crazy he left the house, shouting "Break a leg!" That's how actors wish each other good luck, you know, but he didn't realize how right he was because when I stood on a stool to get a look at myself in the high-up mirror in my husband's workshop, I fell and broke my ankle. Nothing could have kept me away from the premiere though, so, at the hospital, I convinced the nurse to have me driven to Shubert's Casino. They carried me all the way across the theater in a gurney, and everyone laughed, I can assure you. That was May 19, 1924, and it was our first big success."

She began singing again and everyone joined in.

Rebecca interrupted:

"I remember that in Groucho's *Memoirs of a Mangy Lover*, he wrote that the Marx Brothers never would have existed if not for you, but I have the impression that you weren't looking for fame for yourself but for your sons. Which would make you different from everyone else here."

"Not at all! I was thrilled when a Broadway musical about me opened in 1970. *Minnie's Boys*, it was called, and it told the story of our early years. If I had allowed Groucho to become a doctor, I never would have been the star of a Broadway show!"

"I'm not criticizing you . . ."

"I know," Minnie stopped her. "You don't realize we didn't have a choice. In our day, women obeyed their fathers and then their husbands.

The only thing left for us was our sons, so we did what we had to for them to succeed: advice, encouragement, training, just like for an Olympic athlete. It was the only way for us to taste. Nowadays, women work outside the home. They don't need to be mothers to exist."

"They're so lucky!" Jeanne sighed. "I would have loved to have a literary career, become a critic or a journalist . . . I was born in the wrong century."

Rebecca wondered what kind of a mother she had been. Not as pushy or ambitious as these women who had preceded her. All she had wanted was for Nathan to share her values, as if through a kind of osmosis he would be the person she had wanted to be herself.

"Women may have greater freedom today, but mothers are always the same everywhere," Minnie opined. "They still tell their sons, 'Put on a sweater; I'm cold!'"

"Do you really believe there isn't a single child who wasn't conceived to conform to a parent's wishes, who is capable of being the person he wants to be without a thought for his parents' ambitions for him?" Rebecca asked.

"Yes, orphans," Jeanne answered in all seriousness.

8

Jewishness Is Generational

Not only is there no God, but try getting a plumber on weekends.

Woody Allen

God exists but is so inconspicuous that I feel ashamed on His account.

Albert Cohen

What I am really interested in is knowing whether God could have created the world in a different way.

Albert Einstein

"How did you instill a sense of Jewishness in your sons?" Rebecca wanted to know.

"In those days, unfortunately, being Jewish was determined primarily by the anti-Semitism that we had to live with daily," Amalia answered. "In Vienna, we had to vote for Karl Lueger, who was elected mayor in 1895, even though he accused Jews of 'unprecedented terrorism.' Many Jews settled in Vienna after the Emancipation Edict came into effect in 1867. Lueger said: 'We refuse Christian oppression and will not allow Austria's ancient Christian kingdom to be replaced by a new Palestine.' I can remember it as clearly as if it were yesterday. He didn't like the fact that thirty percent of students were Jewish, almost half of the lawyers, doctors and bankers, as well as many artists. Whether they were baptized or assimilated changed nothing in his eyes: 'It's their race that's obscene,' he used to say. He was reelected."

Amalia was still stunned by the mix of superficiality and lurking anxiety that had been the norm in Vienna. Like many Viennese, she was passionate about the arts. People were ready to come to blows over who was the more talented between Arnold Schoenberg or Gustav Mahler, and they traded the latest books by Schnitzler and Hofmannsthal and discussed them endlessly.

"Nevertheless, the political atmosphere was oppressive; you always felt you didn't belong," she continued. "Sigmund had to wait seventeen years to become a tenured professor, even though he had published numerous scientific articles and a half-dozen books. By that time, he had already laid out the proof for his theory of male hysteria, he had invented the 'free association' method, developed his theory of seduction, which he would later abandon, described the Oedipus Complex and discovered the importance of dreams. Despite all that, he remained a lecturer at the university, which was a bitter pill for him to swallow."

"Was anti-Semitism the cause or were his theories on sexuality too shocking?"

"Both, but you have to realize that, when he started at the university, he hadn't done anything to be named professor because he thought it would come naturally. He finally had to contact some influential friends and still he had to wait sixty-four years to receive the official title, the same year he stopped teaching."

Mina appeared, wearing a particularly flattering light pink suit. She looked younger somehow. She suggested they all go out for a while; she couldn't stand sitting all day and she needed some exercise.

"Go out? Where?" Rebecca asked, surprised by the idea.

"Do you like the forest?"

Rebecca followed her into a dense wood of oak and beech trees. She was so happy to be walking in nature that she had a hard time concentrating on what Mina was saying.

"I don't mean to wrongfully compare my Romain to Sigmund," she was explaining. "But my son was also the victim of latent anti-Semitism because he was the only one in his graduating class at the military academy who did not make sub-lieutenant. They said he hadn't been French long enough after his naturalization. He could never bring himself to admit it to me, for fear I would be hurt; I still held such an idealized vision of France. He spared me that."

"What did he tell you? That he had failed his exams?"

"No, he never could have made me believe such a thing. I was sure he was a genius. So, he made up a story about how he had seduced the lieutenant's wife, who then refused to promote Romain out of jealousy. He knew I'd like a love story!"

Amalia slowed down as she tried to give them a better idea of the virulent anti-Semitism that reigned before the war, while avoiding the many clichés that had been tossed around.

"We lived with the constant threat of reprisals and a diffuse fear as more and more Jews fled the pogroms in Russia and arrived in Brody. We accepted them like storms and hail, with a kind of fatalism, like everyone in the ghettos of Eastern Europe, I suppose. Sigmund couldn't tolerate it, though. His father had told him a story that had completely shaken him: 'Once, when I was young, in the same city where you were born, I left the house one Saturday, in my good clothes and wearing a new fur hat. A Christian jumped out at me and knocked my hat off my head and into the mud, yelling: "Off the sidewalk, Jew!"' 'What did you do?' Sigmund asked. 'I stepped off the sidewalk and I picked up my hat,' Jacob answered him calmly. His reaction horrified Sigmund, who never forgave his father for letting himself be treated that way."

"That might explain why he identified later with Hannibal, who swore to avenge his father's defeat by the Romans," Rebecca said. "He wanted to repair the humiliation Jacob suffered."

They were following a stream that meandered through the forest. It was a delightful walk, and Rebecca let herself be dazzled by the play of light through the leaves. It reminded her of the daydreams she indulged in while her students were taking an exam and she could gaze uninterrupted at the sun bouncing against the window of the lecture hall. She was seized by an irresistible urge to run off by herself and stretch out in the grass.

"And how would you define being Jewish today?" Mina asked.

"My Jewishness is no more than a facet of my identity," Rebecca ventured. "I never taught Nathan a thing about religion or Jewish tradition. The best I did was give him a Jewish name: Nathan Rosenthal."

"He never talked to you about what it meant for him to be Jewish?"

"Well, I know he had a very different experience of it than when I was his age. I used to feel that being Jewish gave me an aura that other people didn't have. I identified with the 'Imaginary Jew,' a concept developed by Alain Finkielkraut, and I derived a sense of importance from our collective past and its famous figures, from the 'Wandering Jew' to the emaciated prisoners of the concentration camps and the victims of the Inquisition. I reveled in my inherited heroism. It's not the same for Nathan, though. He doesn't deny his ethnicity; it's just not interesting to him. So he's left to find his place between the anti-Semites he meets, the anti-Zionists who think Israel is a dirty word and his friends who reproach him for not being involved enough in the community."

"That sounds like Romain," Mina observed. "Whenever anyone asked him what his position was on Israel, he used to answer: 'I like Italy a lot, too!'"

"I thought he was proud of his Jewish identity," Rebecca countered. "Wasn't he furious that he wasn't included in the *Who's Who in World Jewry* even though he had filled out the application? If I remember correctly, he also accused the editors of giving themselves the right to decide who 'got sent to the gas chamber.' It's hard to imagine a more violent comment than that."

Amalia wasn't participating in the conversation. She seemed to be engrossed in the walk, striding firmly ahead and leaving Mina struggling to keep up. The group arrived in a clearing, ringed by a circle of benches where they all sat down to rest. Amalia caught her breath to speak.

"Sigi thought of himself as a Jewish nonbeliever, and he was astonished to find himself held up as a Jewish hero when his only merit was that he never denied his Jewishness."

Mina felt she had to clarify: Romain Gary thought himself as Jewish only in reaction to anti-Semitism. He wrote that it was the Shoah that made most assimilated Jews realize that they were Jewish in the first place.

"Sartre said the same thing, didn't he? Anti-Semitism is what defines a Jew," Rebecca agreed.

Amalia interrupted:

"That may be, but Freud said it before Sartre: He was a German by language and culture but, faced with anti-Semitic bias, he preferred to call himself Jewish."

"Was your Jewishness just a way of defining yourselves or did you believe your faith and practice it?" Rebecca asked.

"I was religious by habit as much as by tradition and I assumed my children would be also."

"I did my best to convince Romain to convert to Catholicism," Mina admitted.

"I've walked far enough," Amalia announced. "You've worn me out. I can't go a step farther. Let's go find Louise Cohen; she knows everything about tradition."

Louise was planting a rose bush when Mina, Amalia and Rebecca came upon her. She was wearing a flower-print apron and had her hair tied back. She looked softer than usual. Rebecca didn't waste a moment to ask her what she knew about Jewish celebrations.

"I always loved *Pessa'h*," Louise said. "The whole family came together, and we were always a big group, since, according to tradition, any passersby should be invited to share the meal."

Louise motioned to them to sit in the shade of an arbor, next to which was a table laden with cakes, fruit, and every kind of drink, hot and cold. It was like a peaceful, timeless oasis. Louise wiped her hands and poured herself a glass of water before offering to serve the others.

"I remember the big house-cleaning that always preceded the celebration. The apartment was immaculate and fresh-smelling, like new. My father-in-law sat at the head of the table and read to us the story of the Jews' exodus from Egypt. It was a solemn moment for him. He spoke in a ceremonious drone, very conscious of the effect he had on everyone."

"And what about your family?" Rebecca asked Amalia Freud.

"We observed Yom Kippur of course, but only occasionally Rosh Hashanah, and sometimes Christmas too. We weren't as observant as the Cohens but it was enough apparently for Sigi to keep the illustrated Bible his father had given him for his whole life."

"Maybe it was just a sentimental attachment."

"Nothing was ever easy with my Sigi, I'm afraid. Jacob, his father, was the first to reject the traditional Jewish ways, as a reaction against his father, who was a very pious Orthodox Jew. So he fled the *shtetl* where he was born and raised, got rid of his caftan and fur hat, and adopted western clothing from then on. He assimilated, but he always felt guilty for what he had done. The Philippson Bible he gave Sigi was meant to anchor his son in a tradition that he himself had rejected."

She asked Rebecca a question in turn:

"What about you? Do you believe in God?"

"I agree with Woody Allen: 'If God exists, I hope he has a good excuse.'"

Rebecca seized the opportunity to ask again if she could meet Woody Allen's mother, sure that she would have some fascinating anecdotes about her son. Minnie Marx came into the garden just in time to intervene:

"There's no need for Nettie to be here. It was my Groucho, after all, who was Woody's inspiration: He stole all his ideas from him."

"Whatever did she do to all of you?"

"I think she didn't care for our company."

Was Nettie paranoid or overly emotional? Minnie wouldn't answer. She said that she would rather talk about Woody Allen than about his mother.

"For example, I love this quote from him: 'If it turns out that there is a God, the worst you can say about him is that basically he's an underachiever.'"

"And Groucho, was he practicing?"

"'My partner is:' That's what he once answered a journalist who asked him the same question."

Rebecca tried one more time: would they please tell her what had happened with Nettie? Wasn't she a Jewish mother like the rest of them?

"I'd love to ask her, for example, why Woody Allen has so much to say about religion."

"I suppose you think his mother understands better than we do the meaning of some of his sayings: 'How can I believe in God when just last week I got my tongue caught in the roller of an electric typewriter?'"

"Not really. You all seem so obsessed with your sons; why wouldn't she be too?"

"Because that's the way it is."

The mention of Nettie Königsberg always put Minnie Marx in a bad mood.

"To tell the truth, Albert was the only real Jew among our sons," Louise Cohen remarked. "He even added an 'h' to Coen to 'make it more Jewish.' He took his Jewishness very seriously."

"And Einstein?"

"Come on! So we're not enough for you!" Minnie Marx protested.

Rebecca tried to defend herself, arguing that Einstein must have had plenty to say about religion; wasn't he an atheist Jew who was raised Catholic?

"Everyone was Catholic, more or less, except the Marx family," Minnie observed. "But that's because we were American."

"It's true," Mina confirmed. "I had Romain baptized so he could assimilate completely into French society. That's just what people did back then. He called himself an unbelieving Catholic."

"I even put Albert in a Catholic school when we arrived in Marseille," Louise Cohen explained. "I really didn't have a choice; it was the best school in town. The sisters taught him to say the 'Our Father,' but they always complained they couldn't convert him; he was so adorable."

Rebecca turned to Amalia:

"Surely Sigi wasn't raised Catholic!"

"No although . . . He did go to mass with Monica Zajic; she was his governess and a fervent Catholic."

"And you let him go?"

"I never knew anything about it."

Rebecca was startled to hear someone calling her name: "Rebecca! Rebecca!!!" The voice was new to her but she followed it. It was coming from behind a door towards it. Finally, she opened it, and found herself in a darkly paneled, formal room with two art deco chairs placed on either side of an enormous fireplace. Where was she? She felt out of place. A grey-haired woman introduced herself: It was Pauline Einstein. Her deep blue eyes seemed to shower Rebecca with sincerity and goodness.

"I wanted to meet you. You seem to be interested in education and religion, and Albert Einstein is fascinating on both topics."

Pauline Einstein looked exactly as she did in the photos Rebecca had seen of her: a square face, hair tied tightly back in a neat chignon and wearing a simple black dress that reached to her ankles.

"We didn't observe our faith either. No ceremonies or Kosher food or synagogue," Pauline Einstein explained. "Hermann, my husband, would have agreed with Jacob Freud: Religion was just a superstition. And like the others, Albert went to a Catholic school in Munich. We were very liberal. When he was ten, however, I brought in a relation of ours to teach him the precepts of Judaism so he would understand his ancestors' faith. He became observant and refused to eat pork. He developed a passionate love of God, in the same way he loved music and nature. His faith was irrational yet very deep."

She fell silent, thought for a moment, then began again:

"I think it was the only thing that made Albert happy. Something like the joy I feel when I play the piano."

"You don't miss it?"

"I still play here."

Pauline smiled like a little girl who has just been caught stealing a piece of cake, her face covered with crumbs. She gestured across the room to an immense grand piano piled high with stacks of sheet music. Rebecca was surprised she hadn't noticed it before. Had she been so captivated by this woman? Pauline intrigued her. She still exuded something of the adolescent: awkward, petulant and wistful.

"When did Albert become an atheist?"

"It must have been when he was around thirteen because he refused to make his bar mitzvah, which was quite a statement at the time. His study of mathematics convinced him that the Bible was not a scientific record. He said, 'I believe in Spinoza's God who reveals himself in the orderly harmony of the universe, not in a God who intervenes in human affairs.' From that moment on, he was categorically opposed to religion. He never changed his mind either. He left firm instructions that he didn't want a religious burial."

"You should join the others," Rebecca urged her. "They were just talking about you; they miss you."

"I've been waiting all this time for Minnie to apologize and until then I can't forgive her. I just can't do it. I need more time; I have such violent outbursts at times. I feel like all my composure has turned to anger. It's not like me at all."

"Is it possible that you're more like your true self in death than in life?"

"I'm not the woman I once was: wife, mother, housekeeper, cook, analyst, nurse, all at once, full of love, compassion, energy and never a hair out of place. It exhausted me but I knew how to manage. I miss the person that I was."

Rebecca also felt entirely different in this strange paradise, but she liked her new self. Here, she was calm and relaxed. Oddly too, she didn't miss a thing, whether friends or lovers. She wasn't constantly losing her temper, or worrying about Nathan. Alive, she had thought it was up to her to make Nathan's decisions for him, even though she possessed neither confidence nor kindness; the two essential traits of a good mother. Here, she was finally at peace with herself. And she hoped that, left to his own devices, Nathan would do fine, maybe even better than if she were still there to watch his every move.

Pauline Einstein took her by the hand.

"Come to the piano. I'm going to play you some of Bach's *partitas*."

Back in the garden, Louise Cohen was trimming the box trees and Amalia Freud was napping while Jeanne Proust, who had changed into a pleated summer dress, discoursed on the education their three sons had received: All of them the products of bi-cultural upbringings.

"Sigmund was Jewish and German, just like Albert, who was torn between his traditional Jewish roots and the westernized man he had become. Marcel was the same; he was the son of a provincial Catholic and a fundamentally Parisian Jew: Me. My children were baptized Catholic, but we never discussed religion at home. They hardly even knew they were Jewish."

Rebecca stretched out on a chaise lounge and listened distractedly to Jeanne, before interrupting her to ask why Pauline Einstein kept to herself.

"It's ridiculous," Jeanne answered. "I miss her."

"What happened? Did you have a fight? I didn't have a chance to ask her."

"What? You saw her!" Amalia exclaimed.

"Did she ask how we were?" Jeanne demanded, her voice sounding sadder than she would have liked it to.

"It's all your fault," Minnie accused Amalia. "You had to insist that Freud was more important than Einstein because he invented a new science all by himself."

"Really? That's what you like to think, but you forget that it was you who made her run off."

Their voices grew louder and louder: everyone was accusing someone else of offending Pauline Einstein. Hoping to put an end to what she considered a futile argument, Rebecca asked them in a loud voice:

"Why are there no other mothers here? Why aren't the mothers of Isaac Bashevis Singer and Philip Roth with us, for example?"

Scandalized, Minnie Marx answered her:

"Didn't you know that Isaac never once wrote to his mother after he emigrated to New York?"

"I thought he adored her!" Rebecca said.

"Yes, Besheve was a strong-minded woman, talented and charming. In honor of her, he created his pen-name from his mother's first name and added a possessive pronoun: Bashevis."

"So? What about it?"

"It was a terribly distressing time for him; he felt he wasn't fit for anything and that suffering was his fate in life. He also had a terrible inferiority complex. His brother, Israël, was a famous writer who had saved Isaac's life by paying his passage to America, to join him. Crippled by remorse and lost in an unfamiliar country, horrified by the shocking news coming from Europe, he was completely unable to write. Not a word in eight years, which, for a writer, must be a record."

"Nothing?"

"It took his brother's death for him to write again. But it was too late; his mother was dead by that time."

"I can see why she wouldn't want to talk about her son with you. What about Philip Roth's mother?"

"Bess preferred to go back to her husband," Amalia explained.

"She was here but then she left?"

"When her husband retired, he never stopped criticizing her. He couldn't stand that she made all the decisions, although that's exactly what she had been doing for the thirty years of their marriage and he'd never complained then. She's the very image of the ideal woman and mother. But he was getting depressed, shut up in the house with her all day. His solution was to shout orders and insult her, she who had always been so gentle. She couldn't take it any more and she died."

"What do you mean? She just died?"

"It happens to everyone."

"I know . . . But what happened?"

"She was sick by then but she wanted to make him happy by going out to a restaurant that was practically next door. She was exhausted but she didn't want to cancel, for fear of offending their friends and disappointing her husband. She had hardly ordered before she was dead."

"You can't possibly mean that the last thing she said was, 'I'll have a green salad.'"

"I don't know what she ordered. The subject never came up."

"What was she like?"

"She was the gentlest of us all, and the most sweet tempered too. She had a heart of gold. Her son Philip described her in her forties, short with black hair that was starting to gray, and expressive brown eyes, thin, attractive and completely American in her ways. He remembers how important a clean, well-maintained house was to her, and how she observed the Jewish traditions out of respect for her family. She cooked kosher, lit the Sabbath candles and followed all the dietary restrictions at Passover. He writes that she hardly ever left her neighborhood in Newark, feeling only at ease among other Jews."

Rebecca noticed that Jeanne was nervously twisting a lock of hair around her finger.

"Do you have a different opinion?"

"She was perfect, of course, but irksome. She was a true petite bourgeoisie, so materialistic!"

"You're just a snob."

"I prefer to be called an intellectual," she said with a smile. "But I don't object."

A few seconds later, she added:

"Not as much as Marcel."

"He got it from you."

Jeanne Proust told a story about how Bess Roth used to be terrified that her children would grow away from her. Philip went to college, frequented *goys* and was in danger of losing his Jewishness. He even became optimistic about the future. For an Ashkenazi Jew, unthinkable!

"He considered himself Jewish at home but a 'citizen' outside, like most of his friends," she added. "We wanted our children to be integrated, assimilated, cultivated and influential in their home country, but we were always afraid they would forget where they came from. I would have been heartbroken if any of my sons had become anti-Dreyfusards. It would have been treason!"

"Luckily, they have their fictional alter-egos to explain their Jewishness for them," Louise Cohen retorted.

They decided to continue their conversation in a neo-Moorish synagogue. It was a dark spot, despite the twelve windows symbolizing the tribes of Israel, but they were happy to be there—Rebecca, Amalia Freud, Louise Cohen, Jeanne Proust and Minnie Marx—to talk literature. Knowing their sons' work inside and out, they could say with complete confidence that they had been good mothers; nothing in their boys' lives or even in their thoughts had ever escaped them. Ignoring the balcony reserved for women, they seated themselves downstairs, near the central aisle.

"Albert always denied it but Solal was his double," Louise began. "He's in four of his novels, and my clever son even found a way to kill him off in *Solal* and then to bring him back in *Belle du Seigneur!* Their lives were so much alike: Solal struggled to integrate Geneva high society and to become a senior official at the League of Nations. You can see, by the way, how important it was for him to be on top," she giggled.

After a moment, she began again:

"Solal is magnificent. He steals everything from his boss, Adrien Deume: His job and his wife. He's torn between the West and the East; one is unfamiliar to him but he is the 'Seigneur' in that world; the other he loves, but mostly from afar. He is ambitious and confident, and at the same time full of self-loathing. He complains he 'is what he isn't and isn't what he is.' He adopts a false identity to find love and turns his back on society as soon as he has risen to its heights. He forces the beautiful Ariane to make anti-Semitic statements to resent her."

"A true case of conflicted identity," Jeanne Proust concluded.

"Just like Gilberte Swann, who becomes Gilberte S. de Forcheville! Swann is effaced by a simple initial, as if she wanted to hide her father's Jewish heritage," Rebecca said.

"Back then, a Jew either was proud of his identity and saw all doors close to him, or he denied it and he rose in society, like the Narrator's spiritual father, Charles Swann, refined, elegant, worldly and loved by all the Guermantes," Jeanne reminded her.

"But Swann changes. Why does the green-eyed, red-headed dandy come back to his Jewishness at the end of his life? Is it his terminal illness, the Dreyfus Affair or anti-Semitic propaganda?" Rebecca wondered.

Jeanne began walking up and down the aisles and answered in a sententious voice that suited their surroundings. In the house of worship in which they had gathered, it almost seemed as if she was preaching.

"Marcel makes Bloch the primary object of his anti-Semitic attack. He's a mannerless second-rate writer who makes a mess of everything. In *The Guermantes Way*, he places his top hat on the floor next to him in Madame de Villeparisis' drawing room and then warns everyone who enters to be careful not to tread on it. A few moments later, he manages to smash a vase of flowers, spilling water all over the rug. He quickly reassures his hostess: 'It's not of the slightest importance; I'm not wet.' He is the stereotypical Eastern European Jew, gauche and eccentric, who speaks Yiddish but, far worse, never assimilates into proper French society. He's ashamed of who he is."

Minnie yawned and admitted that she never could read Proust.

"It's not that I didn't try," she explained in her defense. "But nothing ever happens! Sorry, Jeanne."

Jeanne didn't trouble herself to answer but turned instead to Rebecca.

"Do you remember the scene on the beach at Balbec? The Narrator overhears a 'torrent of imprecation against the swarm of Israelites' who have overrun the seaside resort. 'You can't go a yard without meeting them ... You hear nothing but, "I thay, Apraham, I've chust theen Chacop." You would think you were in the Rue d'Aboukir.' Turning around, the Narrator is astonished to discover none other than his old friend Albert Bloch, repeating the same injurious curses that others had used to slander him. He concludes that Bloch is an 'ill-bred, neurotic snob.' Since he belonged to a family that was held in scorn, he had to find the fastest way possible to rise in society. 'To carve himself through to the open air by raising himself from Jewish family to Jewish family would have taken Bloch many thousands of years. It was better worth his while to seek an outlet in another direction.' He found it with the Guermantes, precisely, where he manages at last to be admitted, under the name of Jacques du Rozier, the name of a perfect English gentleman. Swann's route takes the opposite track entirely.

"No one ever called Proust an anti-Semite," Rebecca observed.

"Oh yes, they did," Jeanne corrected her, her cheeks flaming from the memory of the abominable, unjustified attacks on her son.

Louise Cohen, sitting down heavily at the back of the synagogue, launched into her own story about the unfair attacks on her son Albert.

"When his play *Ezechiel* was published, he was criticized for his depiction of two characters. There is Jérémie, a pathetic little schemer who, desperate for money, agrees to go to Ezechiel to inform him of his son's death, although he doesn't know how to go about it. There's also Ezechiel, a rich banker from Cephalonia, the archetypal greedy Jewish moneylender. Albert first describes him deep in some complicated calculations about how to save on candles and he concludes that the seven-branched menorah is the ruin of the chosen people; a three-branched one would have done just as well. Well, you can't imagine what people said! When the play was produced for the first time at the Comédie Française in 1933, it incurred universal wrath: not only the anti-Semitic organizations who saw this as thinly-veiled praise for Jewish values but many in the Jewish community were up in arms, too, because they thought the play was deriding those same Jewish values."

"And when there was a new production of *Ezechiel* in the 1980s it was the object of more of the same outrage, directed again at its depiction of Jewishness," Rebecca added. "It's hard to say though what exactly everyone found so offensive; it seems to me that Cohen was more generally interested in the vulnerability of his 'human brothers.'"

Lost in a Proustian flood of memories, Jeanne merrily continued her own stream of thought, explaining that Bloch's uncle, Nissim Bernard, was comfortable in French society but not what you would call assimilated since he never stopped referring to himself as a Jew.

"Your Nissim Bernard is a perfect example of what was happening in America at the time," Minnie interrupted her. "Christians and Jews hung out together but never married, yet they all considered themselves American. When I lived in New York, every community had its neighborhood: Little Italy, Chinatown, Yorkville.

"You're becoming nostalgic," Rebecca couldn't resist noting.

"I can still remember an old man who only spoke Yiddish. He was moving, and I asked him how it was going, thinking he had just arrived. I couldn't believe it when he told me he had already been in New York for ten years. 'Why don't you speak English?' I asked him. You know what he answered?: 'What for?'" And she laughed and laughed ...

"Wasn't every author who wrote about Jews accused of being anti-Semitic?" Jeanne asked.

Rebecca remembered how Isaac Bashevis Singer was criticized for caricaturing his own people as "Jewish thieves and Jewish prostitutes." His reply was: "Shall I write about Spanish thieves and Spanish prostitutes? I write about the thieves and prostitutes that I know." If the thief was Jewish, why should the reader infer that all Jews were thieves? It is absurd.

Minnie Marx got up suddenly, stamped loudly and shouted for silence.

"I've had enough of your books and all your complicated characters. Your sons might have written pages and pages about how Jewish they were but I'll tell you one thing: It's the food that makes a Jew, first and foremost."

9

I Know What's Best for You

Self-control, sobriety, sanctions — this is the key to a human life, saith all those endless dietary laws.

Philip Roth, *Portnoy's Complaint*

Heaven's kitchen looked so old fashioned that it was hard to imagine anyone could cook in it. A closer examination revealed, however, that even a professional chef would find it more than serviceable. In fact, it had everything! There were two huge stoves, several work counters, and copper pots of every size hanging on the wall from smallest to largest, as well as a full complement of every kind of cookware and utensil imaginable: frying pans, baking tins, peelers, slicers, graters, mincers . . . Minnie, Louise, Mina, Amalia and Jeanne had taken it over. And as usual when no one dared interrupt her, Minnie had monopolized the conversation.

"My mother was obsessed with what we ate," she recalled. "It was only later that I understood why: She watched us to make sure we wouldn't swallow anything that was forbidden to Jews. However, it was also a way of treating us like children. She decided when and what we ate and if we didn't finish everything on our plates, we were punished. She made us feel so guilty! She would say that we didn't love her enough if we didn't eat up. Every meal was a scene because my brother, Al, refused to bend to her tyranny. He would spit into his napkin the bits that he couldn't force down. Sometimes, my mother would grab his napkin before he'd had a chance to flush the evidence of his crime down the toilet. Then she would fly into a rage and make him sit at the table with all the lights out. Sometimes he would be served the same plate for breakfast. Me, I just shoveled it all down."

"Was she the one who played the harp?" Rebecca asked.

"Oh yes, and she took it very seriously, I can assure you, just like food. It's her fault I never learned how to cook: She wanted to control everything."

The food neuroses Minnie had to face in her mother's house put Louise in mind of a Philip Roth book she loved (she had become a big fan of his). In the beginning of *Goodbye Columbus,* Aunt Gladys tortures her nephew at dinner: Why doesn't he want any bread? She brought it to the table just for him! He stuffs himself with bread to make her happy but she keeps at him. Isn't the meat any good? He assures her it is. Then why does he only eat bread and potatoes? Is he trying to hurt her feelings? What a waste if she has to have to throw out all that good meat! Every uneaten carrot and pea is proof of his ill will. Neil Klugman has no choice but to clean his plate; she could have kept him there for hours.

Minnie didn't know the book; in fact, she hardly ever read. She neither had the leisure nor the inclination. She was just too busy to live vicariously through other people. No sooner did she open a newspaper than she fell asleep; it didn't matter where she was, at home or on a train. After missing her stop on more than one occasion, she vowed to never again bother: watching the scenery go by was much more edifying than some journalist's opinion about things that didn't matter. The only books of any use were cook books, which she collected for her husband.

Louise Cohen opened the cupboards one by one, hoping to find inspiration. What could she make? She no longer knew what she liked to eat; she had always cooked for Albert alone, treating him to the richest, most intricate dishes she could dream of. Since he was borderline anorexic, getting him to eat was a full-time job.

Rebecca observed that meals figured prominently in Cohen's novels.

"There's his famously bulimic character, Nailcruncher; his name alone says everything about the ogre he is: he refused to get out of his mother's womb. 'I'm not one to leave a dining room by choice, you know. They had to pull me out of there with pliers,'" Louise quoted from memory. "That's a good one, isn't it?"

"Well, you can laugh all you want about your plate-pushing mothers," Mina interrupted, exacerbated by the stereotype. "It's easy when you're not starving. Romain was touched by the sacrifices I made for him. He understood that every steak I served him was a victory over adversity. My day was never wasted if Romain ate his fill. Once, he walked in on me in the kitchen, licking the sauce right out of the pan where I'd sautéed his meat. I'd always pretended to be a vegetarian. He realized I'd been depriving myself for him. He ran out, ashamed, and he put the story in *Promise at Dawn*."

Louise was lovingly preparing a batch of meatballs while Mina tackled a recipe of that most mythical of Jewish dishes: Gefilte fish. They were putting heart and soul into the job, obviously relieved by having something practical to do. They were the only ones who could find their way around a kitchen, although Jeanne Proust wanted them to know she was highly skilled at drawing up balanced menus. Rebecca, for her part, had always been afraid of food, which was synonymous in her mind with calories—and extra pounds.

"I was convinced I was fat," Rebecca admitted.

"You?"

The other women burst out laughing; by the standards of their day, Rebecca was scrawny.

"Albert was forever telling me how fat I was," Louise remarked, her hands deep in a bowl. "But knowing that I loved to eat, he encouraged me anyway; my unfulfilled desires would make me gain weight, too, he said. That was kind of cruel, don't you think?"

"The subject never came up in our house," Jeanne countered. "Hygiene alone mattered; it was a new concept, and Adrien's speciality, after all. We had to wash our hands before and after every meal. If Robert put up a fight, he'd get a spanking."

"My mother was convinced that what we ate had a direct influence on our health," Amalia Freud told them. "We were a big family, and my brothers devoured everything they could get their hands on. That we had enough to eat was important to my mother but not the main thing: we had to eat healthy."

"Kosher food is very good for you," Louise reminded them.

Rebecca didn't dare join in the conversation. She was fascinated by what they had to say about the rituals around food, which sounded much more complicated than putting ingredients together.

Mina suddenly let out a cry of indignation:

"Sugar! You can't put sugar in that!"

She repeated her exclamation, wide-eyed, to the entire group:

"She can't put sugar in the meatballs!"

Mina hadn't let on but she had been carefully watching Louise at work: ground beef, chopped onions, raw eggs, salt and... sugar. She stopped her with a hand on her arm.

"Russians put pepper in, but never sugar! It's heresy!"

"According to you! Everyone knows that Russian and Lithuanian Jews are uncivilized!" Louise retorted.

"You can keep your Sephardic meatballs to yourself!"

Jeanne jumped into the fray to stave off a fight:

"Some cooks even add powdered almonds. Why don't you each make your own version and we'll decide which is better?

"You're a competitor, Jeanne, and you're always looking for a match off," Minnie answered her. "You know just as well as I do that taste is hardly objective. Everyone will vote for what they know because we prefer the familiar: We're always looking for our childhood in what we eat. Do you know the joke about the new bride who's driven nuts because everything she cooks her husband criticizes? She tries everything, looks all over town for the best ingredients, pores over every recipe she can find, but nothing helps. One day when she's utterly exhausted by her efforts, she leaves the sauerkraut on the stove too long and burns the whole thing. 'Finally! It's exactly like my mother used to make!' her husband exclaims."

"Isn't that the idea of Proust's Madeleine?"

"Marcel was surprised how that little cake could bring back the memory of his Aunt Léonie and, by extension, his childhood at Illiers," Jeanne agreed.

"Oh! Could you find the passage for me?" Rebecca asked her. "It's been so long since I've read it."

Jeanne handed Rebecca the precious volume that she always carried with her, and she read out loud: "'But when from a long-distant past nothing subsists, after the people are dead, after the things are broken and scattered, still alone, more fragile but with more vitality, more unsubstantial, more persistent, more faithful, the smell and taste of things remain poised a long time, like souls, ready to remind us, waiting and hoping for their moment, amid the ruins of all the rest; and bear unfaltering, in the tiny and almost impalpable drop of their essence, the vast structure of recollection.'"

"Isn't that magnificently written?" she asked with tears in her eyes.

Everyone agreed, even Minnie, who had to admit that reading Proust out loud made it all. *Remembrance of things past* an easier pill to swallow.

"Marcel was a finicky eater and ate like a bird," Rebecca recalled. "Céleste Albaret, his chambermaid, said that he never took more than a coffee and a croissant when he woke in the middle of the afternoon."

"Oh, how I tried to get him to eat correctly and have regular meal-times!" Jeanne protested.

"What's interesting is that, once you passed away, he sometimes bought a filet of sole or a sorbet to bring back the memory of taste he had loved in his childhood. Was it for his novel or for himself? I always wondered."

"Both, perhaps."

Rebecca was lost in thought. People's relationship to food is never simple; it's less about what we eat than what food means to us. The foundations are laid in childhood, beginning with our favorite tastes and our revulsions. It's also a means of transgression or disobedience that can take on tyrannical proportions. Nothing breaks a mother's heart more than when her child refuses to eat a meal she has lovingly prepared. Nathan was very fussy about never letting food touch on his plate: he found it disgusting. Meat and vegetables had to be kept separate, and he even went so far as to change plates while he was eating.

Louise Cohen was reminded of a scene in *Portnoy's Complaint*:

"There's the time where Alex is ready to break every Jewish law to escape from his controlling family: he devours a lobster while fantasizing about a *shikse*, a Gentile temptress. Neither one is the least bit kosher!"

When the meatballs were ready, it was time for the mothers to vote on which batch was better, but having devoured them both in two minutes flat, they were no closer to deciding. Minnie finally ventured that, if she absolutely had to choose—and who said she had to, anyway?—she preferred the salty version: in other words, Mina's recipe.

Horribly offended, Louise Cohen jumped up and, without a word, locked herself in the bathroom.

Jeanne and Mina pounded on the door, begging her to come out. There was no response. Minnie tried clumsily to patch up the situation. Really, Louise's recipe was every bit as good as Mina's, and Albert would have been so proud of her.

"Leave her alone," Jeanne ordered, finally. "She's following her son's example. He writes in *O Humans, My Brothers*, that he would have given anything for the restroom attendant at the train station to leave him in peace to do what he had come to do there. But the woman was indignant: how long could it possibly take, she wanted to know. Would he be finished today or tomorrow? Did he think he was in church?"

The door finally opened and Louise appeared, laughing heartily.

"I had forgotten that scene in the restroom! That reminds me again of Sophie Portnoy, who follows her son right to the bathroom where he's trying to masturbate. He shouts at her that he's sick just as he is overcome by a wave of the most exalted feeling of freedom. She begs him to let her in, but he doesn't answer. She tries a more specific line of questioning: had he eaten french fries or—horror of horrors—a hamburger? She uses the same tone of voice as if she would speak of Hitler. She forbids him to flush the toilet so she can scrutinize the contents and she makes him promise never to eat out again, doing her best to pour on guilt. His father, constipated, is the next one to seek peace and quiet in the solitude of the bathroom but Sophie is hysterical and she berates him."

"We could probably write an entire treatise on 'bathrooms in literature,'" Rebecca suggested.

She turned to Jeanne: hadn't Proust described the "little room that smelled of iris" in *Swann's Way* as a good place to masturbate? To get any privacy, Marcel had to hide in the wild-currant bushes.

"You were always watching over his every move," Rebecca reproached Jeanne.

"Don't pretend you didn't behave exactly the same way with Nathan."

"Certainly not. I never paid attention to how much time he spent in the bathroom, nor did I insist, when he traveled, that he write me daily to describe every detail. He could never have written, as Marcel did to you: 'My exquisite little Mother, let me tell you first of all that my stomach is splendid.'"

"You can't know how it was. My son was ill, and we wrote each other even when we lived under the same roof."

"It sounds to me like you were an authoritarian and a possessive tyrant."

"Of course, that's what you'd like to think. In fact, it was just the opposite: Marcel exhausted me. He would throw jealous fits. Take, for example, one of his famous letters, where he beseeches me not to wait up for him to come home from his dinner party, at the same time telling me how delighted he will be to kiss me goodnight. But then he adds: 'Don't come for me. Alas! I saw how you ran toward my aunt with a warmth that you've never felt for me.'"

"Nathan never needed me that way, thank God. On the contrary, he hated having to depend on me and was always trying to assert his independence."

"I suppose he was never sick, like my poor darling?"

10

Sick and Tired

I always thought that as long as man is mortal, he will never be relaxed.

Woody Allen

"In *Remembrance of Things Past*," Jeanne began, "Marcel describes his first and most terrifying asthma attack, which struck him in the Bois de Boulogne. He was ten years old and he would never forget it. I can still see him gasping for air, suffocating, waving his arms, wracked by convulsions. His father and the Professor Duplay were both there too, but neither could do a thing for him. Can you imagine what my little wolf must have been going through? He was about to die right in front of his father and his friend the surgeon? As for me, it was agonizing to discover that, far from being the all-powerful mother I had believed myself to be—I had always managed to calm his night terrors—I could lose him! It seemed like hours before he began to cough again, finally breathing and getting his color back. From then on, we lived in fear of another attack that could strike anywhere, anytime."

"Yet, his father always denied he suffered from asthma. Proust wrote: 'Papa tells everyone that there is nothing wrong with me and that my asthma is a pure figment of my imagination.'"

"There were plenty of theories about what was wrong with him. Some said he was exaggerating, that it was psychological and that I was the problem, which is completely absurd! Marcel continued to have attacks after my death. His illness consumed his entire body. Sometimes, he had difficulty recovering from his attacks, which left him trembling, sweating and out of breath. You have to remember that it was the asthma that killed him at fifty-one."

"So he didn't die of complications of pneumonia?"

"His lungs were worn out from the asthma."

As both the wife and the mother of doctors, Jeanne considered herself to be one too, as if she had soaked up their knowledge by osmosis. As soon as any conversation turned to illness, she adopted an authoritarian air, the better to impose her analysis. Rebecca wasn't ready to give up yet, however:

"I'm not inventing his reputation as a hypochondriac! Didn't he write you in black and white: 'I prefer to suffer from attacks and to have your favor than to have neither attacks nor your favor'? As if he could order his body to do as he pleased!"

"Your insinuations try my patience. I wish he had never written that for all the world to quote and comment on. My own panic over his condition had no effect on his cure. So much the worse! He would have had the health of an Olympian if I had had a say in the matter. Can any mother bear to see her own son suffer? None that I know."

"Nevertheless, Marcel seemed to use his asthma to get what he wanted from you. Maybe he saw that you weren't as strict with him when he wasn't feeling well? He wrote: 'The truth is that, as soon as I'm better, everything in my life that makes me feel well exasperates you, and you destroy it all until I'm sick again.' And he adds, 'It is a sad thing not to enjoy both love and health at the same time.' It certainly seems that his bouts of illness were designed to make you happy, so that you could coddle him as if he were still a little boy."

"Do you really think one can simply choose to get better? I despise this modern theory that illness is all in your head and that the sick simply don't know how to express themselves, or how to be happy or that they lack the will to get better; that sick people are just healthy people who have allowed a virus or cancer or depression or mental illness to take root in their bodies like weeds on a lawn."

Jeanne let her anger fly when she felt backed into a corner. Listening to her, Rebecca realized she was probably the first person who had ever questioned her on the sensitive subject of her son's health. She gave Jeanne some time to calm down by opening Robert Proust's thesis on the female reproductive system. She hardly understood a thing.

Jeanne leaned over to get a better look:

"It's terribly dry. I never managed to finish it and I'm his mother. No need to force yourself, Rebecca."

"What was Robert like with his brother?"

"Adorable. As a doctor, he didn't know how to help him, but there were no known treatments for asthma at the time. Nevertheless, he tried everything in his power to find a solution. He wasn't as driven in this as Adrien was, who couldn't forgive himself for his powerlessness: what good did it do to be a doctor if he couldn't cure his own son? Adrien reproached himself at first, before deciding Marcel was an impossible patient: he went out too much, drank too much, slept too little and did whatever he liked. He tried indirectly to change his behavior by railing against a life of social obligations, in *Hygiene for Neurasthenics*, calling it a 'possible cause of excessive fatigue.' He even used Marcel as an example, writing: 'Neurasthenia is often the legitimate but regrettable price to pay for inactivity, laziness and vanity.'"

"Did Marcel have anything to say about that book?" Rebecca asked.

"It was never published, but my little wolf was highly skeptical about the power of medicine and would take no one's advice. He preferred to spend his father's money, which made Adrien apoplectic with rage."

"What did you think?"

"That he was a spendthrift? Undeniably. Why did he feel the need to give exorbitant tips to waiters? Was it to impress his friends or to get a better table in the restaurant?"

"You can't see the forest for the trees. Did it never occur to you that he acted from generosity and altruism?"

"You have no right to criticize me," Jeanne shot back. "I'm sick of being called stingy."

Rebecca apologized; she didn't know why she instinctively took Marcel's side. Jeanne was irreproachable; all she had ever tried to do was to raise him properly.

But Jeanne was exhausted by their argument.

"In the end, it's true: I criticized Marcel for his lifestyle, the stink of his fumigation powders, and his homosexuality. I never said it outright because he was too sensitive and emotional. Still, he knew what I thought."

Jeanne picked up her book, tired of talking about her son's illness, which still affected her keenly.

Rebecca, leaving Jeanne alone with her thoughts, walked until she came to a bedroom draped in a bordeaux-colored toile de Jouy. Amalia Freud was there, lying in a four-poster bed covered with a thick damask bedspread. Sick and tired, she had no more strength even to move. Her hair was undone and spread out over a pile of pillows. She let her eyes close from time to time, lethargic and mournful. Louise Cohen was at her side, administering cod liver oil and enjoying "playing nurse," as if Amalia was her little doll. Weakened by her pregnancies, she was inclined to take to her bed.

Rebecca hesitated, not wanting to intrude. She had the feeling she was in a Woody Allen movie, with his nerve-stricken, childish, narcissistic characters obsessed by their health. She called them to mind, one by one. There's Mickey, in *Hannah and Her Sisters*: a chronically depressed radio producer for whom the slightest scratch is enough to drive him to suicide. Panic ensues when he thinks he has a brain tumor but, after an initial feeling of euphoria when he learns he doesn't, he sinks into an even deeper depression without his old existential crisis to occupy him. Worst of all is his new knowledge that a life-threatening illness could strike him down at any moment; waiting for death and its unanswered questions frighten him more than even the most terrible affliction. In *Broadway Danny Rose*, a luckless talent agent named Danny is a hypochondriac who is afraid of the outdoors, water and death. In *Hollywood Ending*, it's Val Waxman, a film maker who had his hour of glory in the eighties but is reduced to filming TV commercials. In Hollywood, people think he's either a maniac or a troublemaker, and anyway a self-absorbed, hopeless hypochondriac. Yet another one! And that's not even counting Ike, in *Manhattan*, who thinks everything will give him cancer, or the protagonist of *Whatever Works*, a Russian doctor who botches his marriage, his Nobel Prize and even his own suicide. All of these characters would understand what Tolstoy meant, as cited by Woody Allen in *Hannah and Her Sisters*: "The only absolute knowledge attainable by man is that life is meaningless." As for Woody Allen himself, he's afraid of everything, never leaving the house without a box of pills for his heart, his arteries, his ulcer, his anxiety . . . He stops eating red meat for fear of having a heart attack and he can't buy a shirt without getting his analyst's opinion. He said that "life is divided into the horrible and the miserable": the horrible are the terminally ill and infirm; the miserable are everyone else. He concludes that, if your lot in life is to be miserable, you're "very lucky."

Louise motioned to Rebecca to sit next to the bed where Amalia was resting.

"How are you feeling?" Rebecca felt obliged to ask.

"Not as bad as usual. Did you know that I was never allowed to complain about my health? Sigi hated it when I was sick."

"That's because he was never ill himself, except at the end of his life, with that horrible cancer of the jaw."

"Are you joking? He was sick all the time! He suffered depression, fatigue and apathy among other things. He was his own most important patient. When he was studying the effects of cocaine, he said it gave him an energy and a euphoria that 'is no more than the normal state of a well-nourished cerebral cortex in a person in good health.' In other words, he considered himself far from healthy."

"Your son used drugs?" Rebecca asked indignantly.

"What a horrible story!"

"I can imagine!"

"You have no idea."

Amalia sat up abruptly, her former fragility forgotten. The fact that she was wearing only her dressing gown didn't diminish the ardor of her passionate defense of her adored son.

"Back then, cocaine wasn't illegal. It was thought to be useful medicinally and was prescribed as a stimulant for the nervous system. Even Coca-Cola contained cocaine until 1903. It was in 1883 that my remarkable son first became interested in it, after reading an article by Dr. Aschenbrandt, who explained how soldiers in Bavaria who had been administered doses of the miraculous coca plant proved to be much more resistant to disease than others who hadn't received any. He obtained a supply of it and observed that he no longer felt fatigue, hunger or pain. He hoped his discovery would bring him fame and fortune, which he needed if he wanted to marry Martha. He had to wait four years. But that's another story."

"He became a cocaine addict? I can't believe it!"

"Absolutely not. He was convinced that it wasn't addictive and he gave some to Martha and recommended it to all his friends, so that people started saying he was a charlatan. His friend, the ophthalmologist Karl Koller, heard about it through Sigi and used it as a local anesthetic for the eyes. Koller was the one who was credited with discovering cocaine's therapeutic uses."

"Oh! That must have been a blow to Sigmund's pride."

"Much worse was the loss of his friend Fleischl, a morphine addict, whom Sigi tried to cure with cocaine. But Fleischl's condition, which was very painful, only got worse, and stronger doses of cocaine didn't help. He finally died. Sigmund felt responsible for this catastrophe, which affected him professionally too."

"Did that get him depressed?"

"Sigmund was always depressed. He was special, you know. He had to be the best at everything: he insisted on mastering even the tiniest details, like how to use a certain coffee cup. In his work, which was of supreme importance for him, he forced himself to keep to an immutably rigorous schedule. He couldn't tolerate any unforeseen changes. Everything was a source of anxiety for him."

Jeanne had been listening from the other side of the room, seated at a desk. She suddenly interjected:

"Sigmund wasn't physically ill, though; he lived a normal life, in fact. My Marcel, on the other hand, had to keep to his room, isolated from dust, germs and flowers."

"The difference is that Sigmund was able to manage his illness," Amalia retorted. "He suffered from constant migraines, which led him to theorize that, rather than fight the pain, it was better to identify with it and let it hover above him. One day when he had a terrible bout of sciatica, he noticed that his beard needed grooming. How could he have let himself go that way? He decided right then and there to give up the luxury of being a patient and to return to the ranks of civilized men."

"If it's willpower you're talking about, Marcel had plenty. Otherwise, how could he have written *Remembrance of Things Past*, weak as he was?"

Seeing that the heated discussion had reinvigorated Amalia, Louise seized the opportunity to make the bed and plump the pillows, humming as she worked.

"Albert Cohen always had his health, at least?" Rebecca asked hopefully. She was getting discouraged by Jeanne and Amalia's rivalry over whose son was sicker.

"On the contrary, it was abominable."

Louise sat on the bedcover she had just smoothed and crossed her legs, prepared to provide a full account of Albert's physical ailments. What made these women think that sickness gave their sons a kind of moral stature?

"I witnessed firsthand the deplorable state of his health when his wife, Elizabeth, lived with me in Marseille, waiting for Albert to send her money to join him in Alexandria. She would show me his letters; they were harrowing, describing his devastated emotional state and depression."

"It's completely normal for someone who is alone and far from the ones he loves to have a good case of the blues. He didn't suffer from a chronic illness like Marcel did."

"And like Sigmund did," Amalia added.

"Albert suffered from nerves, insomnia and anxiety his whole life," Louise declared in a loud voice, as if her son's honor was at stake. "As a student, he had all these bizarre obsessions. One of them prevented him from chewing his food, so he could only eat a liquid diet, or purees. He felt as if using his jaws would kill him."

"Freud would have found his case interesting," Rebecca mused. "I wonder what he would have thought of such a strange fear."

"Well, he would have detected the deleterious influence of his mother, for starters," replied a freshly dressed and made-up Amalia.

"I was terribly worried," Louise remembered.

"I was more worried for Marcel than you ever were for Albert," Jeanne countered.

"How do you know? Albert was as asthmatic as Marcel, and depressed on top of it. He suffered from what he called his 'black days' right up until his death. His daughter remembers in *Book of My Father* how he would go for long periods when he never came out of his room, never writing a word or seeing anyone, not even his wife and daughter. They could only talk to him through the door and leave his meals on a tray for him."

"I suppose it's normal to worry, even excessively, about one's children," Rebecca concluded. "We do everything we can for them to be happy."

Louise Cohen remembered Philip Roth's hysterically funny description of Sophie Portnoy, terrified by the unusual symptoms she has observed in Alex.

"Let me read you a passage," Louise insisted, pulling a copy of *Portnoy's Complaint* from her pocket: "'Open your mouth. Why is your throat red? Do you have a headache you're not telling me about? . . . Is your neck stiff? Then why are you moving it that way? You ate like you were nauseous, are you nauseous? . . . Your throat is sore, isn't it?' And it goes on and on."

"I never had to invent any illness for Marcel," Jeanne volunteered, evidently feeling that the specter of Sophie Portnoy had been raised to caricature her own anxiety about Marcel.

They had all been "sick": the asthmatic Marcel Proust, the neurotic Woody Allen, the depressive Romain Gary, the neurasthenic Freud, and the obsessive, insomniac, anxiety-ridden Albert Cohen. Nathan had nothing wrong with him. Unlike these mothers, Rebecca hated it when Nathan was sick. It wasn't that she didn't want him to suffer; she just didn't want to hear him complain. The faintest moan was an affront to her sense of being a good mother; any pain that he felt would have been proof of her ineptitude.

Why did all these geniuses suffer from illness? Were their mothers to blame? Was the cause psychological? A natural narcissist, Mina was convinced that everything was her fault, even Romain's depression.

"Mothers are certainly an important factor in their children's health but it would be wrong to assume we're responsible for everything," Rebecca argued.

"Nevertheless, it was Romain who worried about my diabetes, and the risk that I could die from a lack of insulin. There was a role reversal; he took care of me as if I were his child."

"But that's not why he became depressed."

"The few times when I saw him ill, he did his best to hide it so I wouldn't worry. It was a tactic he used his whole life. His first wife, Lesley Blanch, told me that one day when he had a terrible tooth ache, she asked him what he was going to do about it, and he said, 'I don't care what happens to me. I hate myself so much that I'll put up with pain and suffering.' It's shocking, isn't it? Why would he detest himself like that? He was so hard on himself when I taught him self-confidence."

"I don't think anyone is ever in good health," Amalia Freud said.

"I've never been sick in my life," Rebecca boasted.

"And what good did it do you? Here you are, dead at thirty-eight, whereas I was sick right up to my ninety-fifth year," Amalia retorted.

They continued the conversation in the living room, where Minnie Marx brought a tray of wine and food, declaring that neither she nor her sons had ever been afflicted with illness.

"As the mother of five boys, I never would have had the time to lavish special attention on any one of them, as Jeanne did with Marcel, answering his every beck and call. Once they realized that, they didn't even try."

"Are you saying that these others were sick on purpose, to have their mother's attention?"

"It's the opposite that's true!" Jeanne insisted, exasperated. "Children do everything they can to escape their parents. As soon as they're born, they're lost to us forever, and every phase they go through in life just confirms it."

"You really think so? You all made it impossible for them to exist other than as an extension of yourselves. Any attempt to escape your authority terrified you, so you preferred it when they were sick and needed you the most. Marcel understood that," Rebecca said.

Her words provoked an outburst.

"How dare you say that?" Amalia cried, indignant.

The younger woman was clearly exaggerating, her opinions were indefensible, and she didn't deserve their affection. Provoking them some more, Rebecca went so far as to remind them of Portnoy, this adolescent in all-out rebellion against his mother, who thought that the only thing he could claim as his own was his penis.

"And," she concluded, "I understand him completely."

Realizing that she had gone too far in her criticism of these women who could never admit they were wrong, Rebecca left the room. She found herself in a place with contemporary furnishings: white walls, low tables, minimal decoration. It was light years from the stuffy, almost sinister 19th-century-style rooms she had been in up until then. She called out to Pauline Einstein to join her. She seemed as her only friend and ally since she knew how overbearing the other women could be.

When Pauline appeared, Rebecca made some comments about the room's style, unable to shake the feeling that she sounded like an annoying academic. She talked to forget her worries, empty her head and to resist her terror at being alone for all eternity. She let loose all her complaints, and Pauline patiently listened.

"Come, let's find the others," Pauline said. Finally.

For the first time since Rebecca's arrival, the living room was completely silent. Rebecca scanned the room: Jeanne was reading, Louise was sewing, Minnie was dozing, her hands crossed over her belly, Amalia was fixing her makeup, and Mina was trying on different hats. Pauline Einstein coughed as she entered, signaling her presence.

"Pauline?" Mina ventured, timidly.

Amalia threw herself into the arms of their long-lost companion.

"We've missed you terribly!"

A brouhaha ensued, with cries of joy and surprise all around and everyone talking at once. The happy confusion allowed Pauline to observe her old friends, who had changed only slightly: Minnie looked younger, while Jeanne appeared to have aged, but Louise was exactly as Pauline remembered her.

Rebecca asked if someone would finally explain to her the reason for their falling out. No one paid her any attention. Worse, they continued talking as if she wasn't even there. Were they still smarting from her comments, which they judged inappropriate and hurtful? Or had Pauline's return altered Rebecca's status among them? Would she be sent away from this private mother's club?

"I'm sorry, Pauline," Minnie whined like a penitent dog.

"I was too sensitive," Pauline conceded gently.

"For far too long."

"Time passes quickly here," Pauline replied.

"Not as quickly as it seems," Rebecca noted worriedly, thinking about the eternity she was going to have to spend in this competition for the best son.

"Surely, it's not so different here," Jeanne tried to reassure her. "When you were alive, didn't you always have the same thoughts, say the same things, see the same people, usually the ones you liked the best? You never ventured outside of yourself. Even if you changed slightly over time, your life was infinitely monotonous."

"With one exception," Minnie said pointedly, looking straight at Rebecca. "Here, we do not have to keep the same company forever."

Minnie and Pauline, the two Germans, hugged and kissed again. Minnie was openly crying:

"I should never have insinuated that Albert, the great Einstein, owed his success to his wife. Especially knowing how you hated Mileva. I had no proof to back up what I was saying."

"So, that's what caused the rift between you!" Rebecca exclaimed.

Minnie gestured to Rebecca to hold her tongue; this was no time to risk offending Pauline again. She had suffered enough the first time.

"I thought it over for a long time," Pauline replied. "It's Albert's fault that Mileva's influence has been over-estimated. In his letters, he makes it seem as if he included her in his scientific research, saying for example, 'our theory of molecular forces.' His use of the possessive pronoun is misleading. 'How happy and proud we will be when we have finished our work on the theory of relativity.'"

"Was she a mathematician?" Rebecca asked.

"She was an excellent one, one of the few women of her generation to be admitted to the Polytechnic University of Zurich. But whereas Albert passed his exams brilliantly, she failed them and then abandoned her studies. She was ambitious, however, and there was never any question of her getting her due. So she tried to measure up to Albert Einstein, to become his equal."

"Did she succeed?"

"In a way. But she never published another academic article after their divorce."

"There was a scandal about their daughter, Lieserl. Did you ever find out what happened?" Jeanne asked.

"Lieserl, the poor child, was born in Serbia in 1902 and disappeared in 1903," Minnie whispered in Rebecca's ear.

"I never saw her, and Albert never spoke of her. Mileva wasn't married to Albert when she became pregnant, and she returned to her parents' house to have the child in secret; an illegitimate child could have ruined Albert's career. No one ever knew what happened; was Lieserl left at an orphanage? Did she die of scarlet fever? There were rumors that she was born mentally handicapped. Oh! My daughter-in-law! She was pure poison, that gimpy Serbian. God only knows what she did with the child!"

Now that they were reunited, it seemed a shame to mourn a baby born in 1903 that none of them had ever known. To lighten the mood, Rebecca offered to regale them with stories of Nathan's love life.

"Why took you so long to tell us?" Jeanne exclaimed.

How could Rebecca admit to these domineering mothers that it was difficult for her to comment, expose, explain, dissect and analyze everything, as they did? Even though she did her best to please them, Rebecca often felt as if they belonged to some kind of sect. She accepted the fact because she enjoyed their company, and—who knows?—maybe she too would one day take the same pleasure as they did from endlessly pouring over the details of Nathan's life.

11

Love Lives

I am only a son. I could never know how to be a father or a husband.

Albert Cohen

A mother's love is a promise made to us at birth that life can never keep.

Romain Gary

Love is kept in existence only by painful anxiety.

Marcel Proust

How can you tell, without a doubt, that someone is in love? The answer is that he glows; somehow, he's different. He might seem to be aware of what's happening around him, but he is consumed by an inner fire. He appears alternately calm and agitated, and his emotional state does not correspond to any reality. No matter how banal and ordinary his life is, suddenly it takes on the utmost importance. When he speaks, it's a struggle to express himself aloud because he is simultaneously engaged in an interior conversation with his beloved, who is the constant center of his attention: what is she feeling, thinking, doing at this moment? Like a schizophrenic, a lover lives in two different worlds.

When Nathan fell in love, Rebecca immediately realized that her son was in the grip of the most intense passion, even though he never said a word to her. She didn't dare question him but tried nonetheless to find out what she could about the girl. She was a bit ashamed of this indiscretion, but she never regretted it. What would she have done if there had been any reason to be worried about the affair? She didn't know since she died not long after learning about Eva.

"Who is she?" Minnie Marx wanted to know.

"Is she Jewish?" Pauline Einstein wondered.

"Is she beautiful?" asked Amalia Freud.

"Elegant?" Jeanne Proust demanded.

Each of them had a different relationship with her daughter-in-law, and for each of them there was one quality in her that mattered the most. This fascinated Rebecca, and it was her turn to question them at length. How often did they see their sons' wives? Did they avoid them? Did they love them? Were they jealous of them? She didn't know how she would have behaved. Would have she been Eva's best friend, her confidante? Would she have told her everything about Nathan or given him the freedom to decide what his beloved should know about him? Would she have been a weight and advise her daughter-in-law on anything and everything? Or would she have let her manage her own family, leaving her to decide what was best? She would never know. Is there such a thing as the perfect daughter-in-law? How had these overbearing mothers reacted to theirs? She turned to Pauline Einstein first.

"Did Mileva know how you felt about her?"

"Of course. I never made any mystery about it. When I wrote to her parents, I discovered that they were unhappy with the match too."

"And yet they married anyway?"

"Yes, but the marriage was doomed from the start. After the wedding reception, when they got home to their apartment in Berne, Albert had lost his keys. Could there be a more obvious sign that he was resisting their life together? A Freudian slip, as Sigmund would say."

"Perhaps he was just distracted."

"Of course," Pauline acquiesced with irritation.

Was Rebecca's direct and critical approach going to antagonize Pauline? Should she stop questioning these women since they were obviously too sensitive to handle it? Should she keep her thoughts to herself?

If she didn't insist with Pauline, though, she'd never know more about Albert Einstein, the lover.

"Did things go better with Albert's second wife?"

"Elsa! She was adorable!" Pauline remembered fondly. "She was already part of the family when she married Albert: her father was Hermann's cousin, but she was also my sister's daughter and my favorite niece."

"You mean, Albert and Elsa were cousins?" Rebecca cried, almost choking with surprise.

"I loved her almost as much as I loved my own daughter," Pauline continued dreamily, ignoring her. "She was an angel."

"Was it a good marriage?"

"It might have been, but Albert was difficult and the bourgeois nest that Elsa built around him hung on his shoulders like an oversized coat. He was always absent, lost in his calculations. I felt sorry for her."

Jeanne Proust changed the subject abruptly, even at the risk of offending Pauline.

"Rebecca, weren't you going to tell us about Nathan?"

"That's right! What was the name of his sweetheart again?" Pauline piped in. It was her way of signaling to Jeanne that she didn't take her interruption the wrong way.

What a difference there was between Pauline Einstein and Jeanne Proust! If she didn't know them, Rebecca would have misunderstood them completely. Pauline's outwardly severe appearance would surely have intimidated her but, in reality, Einstein's mother was maternal and protective. It was as if her difficult life had rubbed off on her appearance. Whereas the cultivated Jeanne Proust, whom Rebecca would have taken an instant liking to, was mercilessly judgmental. It was her courtesy that led you to believe—mistakenly at times—that she was interested in you and liked you. Both women were fascinated by Nathan's story, though, almost as if he were one of their sons. Rebecca concluded that she had finally been accepted into their group.

"Eva is Nathan's age. She's studying finance and loves mergers and acquisitions. She's intelligent, independent, happy, energetic and apparently she adores my Nathan. I never expected I could be so happy for him."

"You don't even know if she's Jewish, do you?" Pauline.

"I couldn't care less."

Pauline Einstein loved Elsa because she was part of her own family, but hated Mileva, who was a foreigner. From that point of view, she was just like Mrs. Millstein, in Woody Allen's *Oedipus Wrecks*, who can't stand her son's girlfriend because she isn't Jewish: how could a *shikse* possibly know how to take care of Mrs. Millstein's darling? She makes their lives hell until the girl's driven out and a nice Jewish one takes her place. Then, she's as charming as she can be with her future daughter-in-law. And showing her photographs of Sheldon from infancy to adolescence, they both go into ecstasies. The poor man has no business being in the same room, even though they are talking about him! His mother swoons, gazing adoringly at his gorgeous, five-year-old face, but the grown Sheldon—though he is a brilliant lawyer—she criticizes and humiliates constantly.

"Isn't that the very definition of love?" Pauline asked. "Isn't it true that we fall in love with the idea of someone we don't even know? Marcel thought so, didn't he, Jeanne?"

Jeanne Proust grumbled an inaudible response, not having the appetite for discussing her son's love life. It was the first time she ever avoided a discussion about Marcel. She preferred to hear more about Eva, whom she disapproved of already.

"You don't even know her last name. She's probably a social climber, ambitious and egotistical. Wouldn't Nathan be better off with a more sensual, full-figured woman?"

"Why are you so pessimistic? If he loves her, it's because she's his type. I prefer to think they share a genuine affinity and that they complement, each other and respect each other."

Rebecca's optimism on this subject at least was unshakeable. Although she had despaired over his idleness by comparison with the other mothers' famous sons, she had learned from the interminable discussions to have faith in his abilities. Now she was convinced that he would be happy and that his wife would love him . . .

"So, you believe in fairytales?" Pauline Einstein asked her, incredulous.

"What makes you so sure of yourself?" Jeanne asked almost at the same time.

A memory flashed before Rebecca. One evening, she found Nathan in his room, seated at his desk, legs stretched out, arms thrown back over his head. He was laughing, smiling, joking: Just happy. His deep voice had thrilled her more than the gentlest words whispered after lovemaking. She was speechless with admiration, looking at him.

"Nevertheless," Pauline insisted. "You can't be happy he's dating a *goy!*"

"He wouldn't be the only one," Louise Cohen answered. "Albert had a weak spot for them too. It's not for nothing that his hero, Solal, tries to seduce every Adrienne, Aude and Ariane he meets, each as magnificent as the next: Elegant, cultivated and refined. Jewish women, on the other hand, are always described as ugly and fat."

Louise Cohen was making a habit of bringing up Philip Roth any chance she had; she recognized in him Albert's own preoccupations with women and Judaism.

"Portnoy slept compulsively with wasps, as a way of conquering America, a little like a man living abroad will prefer to have a mistress who speaks the local language rather than study it in a book."

"It's a crime not to respect one's origins," Pauline Einstein said angrily. "Our people's survival is at stake."

Rather than respond to Pauline and defend Nathan, Rebecca decided to find out more about Albert Cohen's adventures in love.

The air was cooler than they expected when they went into the garden. It was laid out in a square surrounded by crenellated walls, and all four seasons were represented: to the north were hardy shrubs and grasses, to the south there was a profusion of fruit trees, to the east, the ground was covered with autumn leaves, to the west, there were spring roses. In the middle was a labyrinth made of plants and flowers, herbs and greenery. It reminded Rebecca of the *Roman de la Rose,* where the rose symbolizes the poet's beloved, whose affections he must earn by completing an arduous apprenticeship in the ways of love.

There were cushions scattered on the freshly cut lawn. Rebecca sat among the others in a circle.

"We can't choose who our sons are going to fall in love with," Rebecca began. "There are limits to what a mother can do. On this subject at least."

"Albert did as he pleased," Louise Cohen replied. "His first wife, Elisabeth Brocher, was the daughter of a Protestant pastor. She died of lymphoma. We enjoyed each other, but I tried to stay out of her affairs, even when she lived with me. I never spoke of Albert with her. It seemed improper."

"How many times did he marry?"

"Three. After Elisabeth, there was Marianne Gross, then Bella Berko-vitch. She was the only one of his wives who was Jewish. He married her after I died, and he found happiness, finally, with her. He said in the last interview he ever gave: 'I'm eighty-five years old and I'm going to die one of these days. But I'm happy to love my wife in my old age and to be loved by her in my old age, and this love that is given and received is all that matters to me.' He loved Bella, and he dedicated *Belle du Seigneur* to her."

In the great romances of the Middle Ages, the courtly lover is set the task of winning his lady through a display of his virtues, of which love is the most supreme. Once smitten, a knight and his lady never worried about what their parents would think!

You never heard what Lancelot's mother thought about Guenièvre his beloved!

Mina admitted she had tried to influence Romain's choice of women. She believed he had found the perfect one: Ilona, whom he wrote about in *Promise at Dawn*.

"We understood each other. We were from the same part of the world. Well, not far, at least. She was Hungarian, Jewish, cultivated, comfortably well-off. Four years older than Romain, he was head over heels and infinitely more besotted than she was. So just before she was to go home to her parents for Christmas, he asked her to marry him. She never returned. Worse still, he lost all trace of her, until 1960, when he found out she had gone mad and had been interned in a psychiatric hospital all those years."

"He was lucky she left him," Rebecca said.

"Maybe so, but he became a womanizer from that day on."

"Isn't that what you loved about him, that he was a lady killer?"

"Obviously. Having many women is the mark of a successful man. Romain himself wrote that it goes hand in hand with 'official honors, decorations, uniforms, champagne, embassy receptions . . .' He was right of course."

"My boys had more lovers than I could count, Chico in particular," Minnie Marx interjected. "I didn't have anything to do with it: just by smiling, the girls swooned. He was a compulsive ladies' man, and it made Groucho jealous."

"He must have been the shy type."

"The title of Groucho's autobiography gives you an idea of how he thought about himself: *Memoirs of a Mangy Lover.* I don't think he was ever happy in love, but it wasn't for fault of trying: he married three times."

"What were his wives like?"

"I never criticized them, but I preferred to see them as little as possible."

"Divide and conquer: was that the strategy for both of you?" Rebecca dared to ask Mina and Minnie. "That way, you never lose your son to another woman; you're still the only woman who really matters to him."

"I have no idea what you're talking about," Mina replied with complete insincerity.

"Nor do I," Minnie declared. "All I ever wanted from my sons were grandchildren."

"Typical. So you were just like Alex Portnoy's parents?"

Rebecca, too, was finding Philip Roth's book to be a useful reference. Unable to get out from under his parents' watchful eye, trapped between his hysterical, castrating mother on the one hand and his repressed and literally blocked up father, Roth's young protagonist waits for the chance to leave his neurotic family behind and see the world, or another part of it than New Jersey, where everyone looks like everyone else. He goes in search of non-Jewish women and non-kosher food, masturbates every chance he gets and struggles to find his much sought for freedom. One of his family's chief complaints is his single status. How selfish not to want to make such wonderful parents happy by getting married and giving them grandchildren! Hadn't they done everything for him? Why didn't he have his sights on a serious young lady? That's what his father always wants to know. After all, he wouldn't live forever . . . and he'd like to get to know his grandchildren before it's too late.

"Did you lay a guilt trip like that on your sons, too?"

"Maybe," Minnie laughed. "If I did, though, my attempts were never as cliched as that."

What could be more egocentric than wanting grandchildren and to care about passing on a family name? It would be even worse if they couldn't stand their daughters-in-law, those unbearable rivals for their sons' attention . . .

"It must have been difficult for you to imagine them happy with their wives and far from your grasp," Rebecca ventured.

"Not in the least!" Mina exclaimed. "We were irreplaceable!"

There is no substitute for a mother, and certainly not a mother such as these; Rebecca ought to have known that. Grumbling and grouching about the cramps in their legs from sitting cross-legged in the grass, they got to their feet. Why were they talking about their children leaving the nest, anyway? Any subject was better than that. They found a new spot to rest themselves, under an arbor in the summer quadrant of the garden. A bower of roses provided shade from the sun and was reflected in turn by a pool of water lilies that looked straight out of a Monet painting.

"Our sons never really went away," Minnie began.

"How could they? Only a mother can know her son's every desire," Mina commented. "She's the only one who can interpret his moods and support him, whatever state he is in. She loves him unconditionally. What's wrong with that?"

"It makes bad habits," Rebecca answered, recalling Gary. "He makes it clear that his mother's love ruined his romantic relationships: 'You believe that you have it in you to be loved, that it is your due, that it will always be there around you, that it can always be found again, that the world owes it to you, and you keep looking, thirsting, summoning.' But it's impossible.

'You spend your days waiting for something you have already had and will never have again.'"

"Is that a criticism, do you think?" Mina asked, worried all of a sudden.

"What's wrong with you?" Jeanne Proust cried. "Could you have acted any differently? You were in an impossible situation, which you met heroically. Were you supposed to stop yourself from loving your son, on top of everything else? Would he have been happier if you had?"

"I don't know," Mina said soberly.

"This is ridiculous, in any case," Jeanne said with an offended air. "How could we ever stop loving our sons?"

Mina was wearing a stunned look; the idea that she might have been a harmful influence on her son was utterly shocking.

"Don't believe for a minute that you sabotaged his love life," Rebecca told her, in all sincerity. "He adored you; you were the center of his attention. He fulfilled your wish for him to become a writer and an ambassador; he longed for your approval. In *Lady L*, when the protagonist is admiring the luxurious apartment where he is living, he says: 'If my mother could see me now!' That says it all."

"If you had been alive when he married Lesley, would you have approved of her?" Jeanne wanted to know.

"Romain fell in love with her independence, her sophistication and her haughty manner. She was forty years old; he was only thirty. But their marriage was ill-fated because it rested on a misunderstanding; she was fascinated by Russia and he was fascinated by France. Both of them were in love with a country that only existed in their imaginations, but it was a different country for each of them. Lesley's Russia was a place of dangerous passions, romantic peasants, sad music, dark tapestries, tragic literature and noble barons. It was nothing like the Russia that Romain fled; the pogroms and poverty he knew were hardly romantic. She thought she was marrying a Russian, but Romain wanted nothing more than to be French. His France was like a heroic, elegant, proud, and beautiful woman. It intimidated an Englishwoman like Lesley. Once she realized that, she became little more than a substitute mother, though not as firm as I was. She educated him, taught him good manners so he could mingle in her world of high society, but she should never have given him so much freedom."

"Maybe it was her own freedom that concerned her. She was hardly going to become a housewife at forty."

"She certainly never expected him to have so many mistresses."

"Since she had her own lovers, why did they separate? They led an exciting life between London, Paris, Sofia and Los Angeles."

"Jean Seberg broke that all up. Romain left the 'mother' for the 'daughter.'"

It was growing darker as the sun set in the sky, but the garden began to glow as lanterns and projectors threw their light upon thickets and climbing ivy and statues.

"Wasn't Albert Cohen's first love also an older woman, like Romain's?"

"Amélie Costa was twenty-six, eleven years older than Albert," Louise Cohen confirmed. "She was a lovely singer who knew how to take care of him. Albert was young and proud to have won her; he liked to show her off to his friends when she picked him up from school in a horse-drawn carriage."

"I thought she was a Hungarian countess?" Rebecca said.

"Oh no! You must be thinking of Béla Fornszek. That was a more serious relationship, and she was older than him too. She was thirty-five when she fell in love with Albert, who was only twenty at the time. He was more like a son than a lover to her and that's how she treated him. She helped him publish his first essays and she introduced him to influential people."

"Just like Romain and Lesley!" Mina was thrilled with the similarity.

Louise began to pace up and down, lost in thought. She had something to say but she was mulling it over. Minnie, Mina, Rebecca, Amalia and Jeanne exchanged silent glances, waiting for her to speak. Louise Cohen sighed deeply.

"If our sons—all of them—were attracted to older women, isn't it our fault? Either they loved us too much or too little; that's what I was wondering. You couldn't say they lacked maternal love!"

"Certainly not!" Mina exclaimed with a tremor in her voice.

Rebecca didn't dare speak, lest she be banned forever from their company. Her theory (she always had one) was that these women never allowed their sons the freedom they needed to become adults. Instead, they were forever seeking their mothers' loving glances: that mirror that always told them they were wonderful. An older woman who was protective, asexual and faithful could give them that. Nothing like the overtly carnal monsters that sickened Solal, who was happy to have an excuse to avoid their company. But illness was only a respite. As soon as he was better, "the life of love" would start again and "the priestess of the swelling jaw muscles would oust the loving mother. Farewell herbal infusions, goodbye lovely poultices!'"

"Freud never fell for an older woman," Rebecca observed.

"That's what you think!" Amalia shot back. "When Sigi was only sixteen, we sent him to rest in Freiberg, where he was born, but there he fell in love with Gisela Fluss's mother, though he never admitted it. He wanted a mother figure, just like Albert Cohen and Romain Gary."

"But was she ever his lover?"

"It doesn't matter if she was," Pauline replied. "The main thing is that he hid his feelings for Eleanor, all the while pretending he was in love with her daughter, who was sixteen, like him. Eleanor was an intellectual and my complete opposite. I was just a housewife and he was ashamed of me. I realized that."

"Why are you so critical of yourself? Sigmund admired you and recognized your power. He tells the story of how, when he was six years old, you explained to him, rubbing your palms together as if you were making knödels so that the dry skin of your hands flaked off, that man came from the dust of the earth and would return to that state. It was a lesson he never forgot."

"Perhaps, but I don't think I was the mother he would have liked me to be. He was always falling under the influence of women who were all very different from me."

"Marcel never replaced me, though he wasn't as complicated as Sigmund."

"More introverted, though," Amalia retorted.

"Are you insinuating something about his homosexuality?" Jeanne asked, feeling vulnerable again.

"No, I was referring to his shyness and his oversensitiveness. His sexual preferences are common knowledge; you shouldn't take offense."

"That's not what pains me, but rather the fact that my little wolf was never happy in love. Marcel knew he would have to leave me if he were ever in love. But that meant risking rejection, and that was impossible for him; it was too frightening. He preferred to stay close to me. He even says in his famous questionnaire that the worst thing that could have happened to him would have been not knowing me."

Amalia Freud was disgusted by Jeanne's contrived concern:

"You made it impossible for Marcel to live apart from you. He was incapable of a romantic relationship because of that. He didn't dare risk your displeasure by showing that he could be anyone other than the person you wanted him to be."

"I can't understand a single word of your nonsense," Jeanne shot back, furious. "I don't care if you think I was a bad mother; you wouldn't be the only one here. But if you're implying that I was responsible for his homosexuality, say it outright. The 'race of aunts' he writes about stretches far and wide. And I'm not referring only to Marcel's fiction, with Vaugoubert, Jupien and Morel, the Prince of Foix, everyone who gravitates around Charlus, Nissim Bernard, the Prince of Guermantes, Saint-Loup . . . He also explores lesbianism at length: Albertine and the girls at Balbec. And how can a mother be held accountable if her child is a homosexual? It's not her fault."

"It seems to me you hide behind what he wrote, and yet you were constantly watching over him, never leaving him any freedom."

"He had me; what else did he need?"

Pauline Einstein was listening from a distant corner of the garden. After having been alone for so long, she shunned group gatherings. Rebecca went to keep her company.

"Albert didn't have as many problems as the others, and it wasn't just because he was absorbed by his mathematical equations," she said. "He knew how lucky he was and never subscribed to the negative perception of love that the our friends' sons over there shared."

Seeing Rebecca's astonishment, she explained:

"Proust and Cohen were as tortured by love as by their own pessimism. They believed no more in love than in marriage or even friendship for that matter."

Rebecca recalled certain passages in *Remembrance of Things Past*, where love is a form of torture, swinging wildly between extremes of frustration and suffering. The examples are as numerous as they are unfortunate. Swann is consumed by jealousy over Odette, and he speaks of his love as of an illness that must be cured, before admitting finally that he threw his life away for a girl who wasn't even his type. He changed his tastes, his friends, his habits, for her: was it worth it? Saint-Loup lies to Gilberte, though he loves her, and the Narrator loses his head trying to keep Albertine to himself. The only happy lovers are the Marquess de Villeparisis and the Marquis de Norpois, but he has much less to say about them. "I must choose, either to cease from suffering, or to cease from loving," Proust writes.

One by one, the others joined them. A candlelit table awaited the assembled party for dinner. The mood was romantic, as if a love potion had been diffused in the air. Louise Cohen wanted to discuss *Belle du Seigneur*, and no one saw any reason to stop her.

"Just like his author, Solal tried to keep the flame of passion alive. True love, the kind that grows and lasts, is a contradiction in terms. My son said so: 'Their words of love had become good manners, a polite ritual, gliding over the linoleum of habit.' He calls Adrien Deume the 'stomach-churner' in *Belle du Seigneur*. He didn't have very high-flown ideas about love, you're right about that, Pauline."

"I don't agree," Jeanne said. "He was skeptical about marriage but he enjoys describing the blazing passion that consumes Solal and Ariane."

"It all finishes badly for them in the end, since they commit a double suicide," Louise remembered regretfully. "The 'sublime delirium' they feel in the beginning becomes a 'prison of love.' Their first meetings, the desire, the waiting, the exaltation: none of that lasts. Solal reveals to Ariane his ten-step plan to seduce her, and still she falls in love with him, just as he had predicted and planned. It's a disaster: he has to keep it exciting, make her jealous, invent problems so as not to succumb to his boredom."

"Cohen describes love marvelously, and no one can deny it," Jeanne countered with immense conviction.

For the first time, Jeanne was taking the side of someone other than Marcel. Did she have a romantic streak, Rebecca wondered? She had held love up as the most sublime sentiment, her voice filling with emotion, and in her agitation, she creased and re-creased the folds in her dress.

"You describe Cohen as a cynic when, in fact, he was an idealist. I was deeply moved by the beginning of *Belle du Seigneur*. I've read it a dozen times, and it's still the most beautiful declaration of love I know. He has won his beloved Ariane and he wants to live a love that is pure and unique and absolute. So he disguises himself as an old, poor, ugly and toothless Jew and he demands her to love him. He believes in her, he does everything in his power to convince himself she will be different from other women. He carries off the subterfuge admirably and he believes for a moment that she loves him too because she says she will kiss him, but she throws a glass at him instead."

"Yes, and he is disappointed to learn that two teeth are all that stand between him and the great love he idealizes," Rebecca agreed. "It seems absurd but it's true. Should that be so surprising? I wonder. We love our children unconditionally, but we choose our men. Love doesn't fall from the sky, no matter what Anna Karenina says to justify her affair with Vronsky. She insists her love is God-given, that they were meant for each other, that it was her destiny to cheat on her husband. Albert Cohen, on the other hand, knows that if Vronsky had been ugly or a man of lesser rank, she would have never looked his way. Anna Karenina is no different than most women, Ariane included: only the strong and handsome will do, not the toothless old men."

Louise Cohen was mesmerized by the vigor of their discussion and the conviction with which each of them argued her point. She followed the exchange of volleys between Jeanne and Rebecca as if she were watching a tennis match. Minnie cut their debate short:

"Groucho was a realist; he held no illusions about love. One of his favorite stories goes like this: a woman tells him she loves him, so he asks her if she would feel the same if he were poor, to which she replies, 'I would, but I wouldn't tell you.'"

In the heat of their conversation, they emptied glass after glass drinking too much.

"Look at Woody Allen's movies," Rebecca said. "They always rest on a communication problem between two lovers. Everything is complicated: boredom, sex, self-esteem. By definition, a relationship is unhappy and deceitful."

There is a scene in *Annie Hall* where Alvy and Annie have just returned to Annie's apartment after a tennis match and are standing on the balcony. Subtitles appear, revealing what they are thinking, as opposed to what they are saying. Alvy is talking about all the photos on the walls of the apartment but he can't stop wondering what Annie looks like naked. Annie is telling him about her photography classes but is ashamed to hear herself talk: An imbecile capable of only the most banal statements, she thinks. Alvy's not listening to a word, though, because he has already fallen for her. Being in love means never having to listen to each other!

"Do you know that Woody Allen joke?" Minnie Marx asked. "A man walks into a psychiatrist's office and says, 'Doctor, my brother is crazy; he thinks he's a chicken.' The doctor says, 'Well, why don't you get him institutionalized?' 'I would,' the brother says. 'But I need the eggs.' Woody tells the joke to describe relationships: 'They're irrational and crazy and absurd, but we keep going through it because most of us need the eggs.'"

Rebecca was daydreaming. Even if she never met Nettie, she would always have the same image of Woody Allen: funny and pessimistic at the same time. Her opinion of Freud, Einstein, Proust and the others had evolved, however, since she met their mother.

Louise Cohen continued to drink, but the alcohol wasn't improving her mood.

"Woody Allen and Marcel Proust are pessimists, but Albert was the most unhappy person who ever lived. He was bored his entire life. Can you imagine what it's like to need to invent stories for your wife just to create some kind of excitement? Like Sheherazade, he knew that his life was nothing if it weren't for the tales he told. So he imagined *Solal* for Yvonne Imer and *Belle du Seigneur* for Bella, but it all started with his first wife, Elisabeth. He insisted on the seriousness of their relationship; he was her lord and she must worship him. And since he would not tolerate any fun and games from her, she stopped talking. There was nothing left for him but to take over the conversation."

"She let that happen?" Rebecca asked.

"Let me read you one of her letters; she describes the awe in which she held him: 'My master and my friend, have you really chosen me to be recreated in your image? The honor is too great, too strong for my humble self.' She admired him unconditionally. But she could hardly do otherwise: he forbade her to have any interests that might distract her from him. Their sex life suffered, too. He says through Solal that he was 'tired of the voracious lips and tongue of women' and he laments about the 'peculiar suction that glues male and female together.' Can you write such a thing if you've never felt that way?"

"You're tough on Albert. Was he really as egomaniacal as all that?"

"He was obsessed by the horrors of conjugal life, the toothbrushes, the flushing toilets," Jeanne continued. "He wasn't the only one who detested all that."

"He would never have had such thoughts if he had loved his wife," Louise replied. "As for me, I can still remember how happy it made me to lie alongside my husband's warm body and to feel our chests rising and falling in unison. Nothing was ever as soothing to me."

"Yes, well, a hot water bottle does the trick just as well," Jeanne.

Louise Cohen was changing physically before their eyes. The more she talked about her son, the more deepened the lines on her face. Dark circles appeared, and her complexion became mottled.

"Albert Cohen was incapable of love," she declared. "One of his mistresses, Jane Fillion, said, 'Albert Cohen never loved anyone except Albert Cohen. But he loved that man with all his heart.' He wasn't capable of any sacrifice or compromise for the simple reason that no one else existed for him. His second wife said as much: 'He denies you even the right to be a human being.' She wore herself out submitting to his demands and then left him, finally. The people he loved had no actual substance. Like Solal says, they were 'dream figures' only."

"In fact," Rebecca began, following a new idea that had just come to her, "*Belle du Seigneur*'s title is saying that the woman loved is both beautiful and belongs to her master. She has neither identity nor substance."

"It's my fault that Albert was impossible to live with," Louise lamented. "I never taught him how to get along with people. For me, he was such a priceless treasure that I used to move out of his way to leave him all the room he needed."

Jeanne was compulsively tidying up the remaining bottles on the table. Rebecca was helping her, but her mind was running over their conversation and the questions it had raised. To what extent were these mothers responsible for how their sons turned out? Why were they all unhappy lovers? What could explain Cohen's tyranny, Proust's solitude, Romain Gary's suffering, and Woody Allen's complexes? They all needed to be loved and reassured. They sought an image of themselves so they would not suffer. The only relationship they could tolerate was one that excluded the other, in a fusional love.

Amalia Freud poured herself a shot of whiskey.

"Sigi demanded constant proof of Martha's love for him, which he always doubted, because he was wildly jealous. He was extremely fond of his wife and believed her to be more powerful than she probably was. How could he compare her to Melusine, a female spirit with total power over her husband? Was it because he feared she would turn him into a weak human being? Sigmund never failed to tyrannize her and, when he felt she had regained the upper hand, he no longer paid any attention to her. He made her life hell because she had to agree with him on everything.

Even her own family had to be sacrificed in her all-consuming devotion to him. He didn't just want her to criticize her mother and her brother but to stop loving them entirely. If she didn't share absolutely everything with him, she no longer deserved to be his wife. I found a letter Sigi wrote to Martha during their engagement: 'Nothing pleased me before I met you, and now that you are mine, in principle at least, my only purpose in life is to possess you completely. If I fail to do this, I hold my life to be of no value.' In the guise of a love letter, he wrote only about himself. It's a shame he never made the effort to see Martha as she really was: devoted, spirited, organized and loving. He didn't know her at all."

Rebecca recalled that Freud spent his holidays with his sister-in-law Minna Bernays, while Martha stayed at home with the children. He claimed he needed these vacations for his health. His intimacy with Minna was a source of speculation, and there exist ample descriptions of the places where they vacationed and the hotels where they stayed. Biographies of Freud usually mention that she lived with the Freuds and slept in a bedroom that adjoined the couple's own, a fact that displeased their daughter Anna.

"Their relationship has been quite thoroughly dissected," Rebecca said. "But were they or were they not lovers?"

Her question upset Amalia.

"Those rumors were spread by Jung after he had a falling out with my son. Sigi was faithful to his wife; he had six children with her, and I can assure you that he had nothing to reproach himself for. He had lunch with me every Sunday; I would have known."

"He stopped having sexual relations with Martha when he was forty," Rebecca reminded her.

"What of it? He was depressed, and sex no longer interested him."

At the opposite end of the garden, Amalia Freud made herself comfortable on a rocking chair. She felt weary and alone. Rebecca and Jeanne soon joined her. They hoped Amalia would be able to tell them more about the complicated relationships Freud had had with his family; they weren't about to let drop such a fascinating subject. Jeanne in particular wanted to know everything there was to know about Sigmund's friendships.

"Freud maintained very close relationships with his friends. Could this be why he stopped paying attention to his wife? He wrote two hundred and ninety-five letters to Wilhelm Fleiss over seventeen years."

"And to think we'll never know if Marie Bonaparte purchased those letters," Amalia replied, avoiding the matter of his abundant correspondence.

"All of his friendships were intense," Jeanne continued. "Breuer, Jung, Adler, Rank, Ferenczi: they traveled together regularly and wrote to each other daily."

"His letter writing began during his four-year-long engagement to Martha. After they married, he looked for other people to write to. He liked to confide his thoughts and feelings to friends in letter form; he claimed it helped him think and see his theories more clearly," Amalia argued in his defense.

"Martha was extremely jealous of Wilhem Fliess, with whom Sigmund had the same close relationship that he had with you. You only have to read his letters to understand the intensity of his feelings for Fliess: 'People like you must never go away,' he writes at one point. Another time, he thanked him for his consoling, his understanding, his encouragement at a time when he felt alone. He added: 'You helped me grasp the meaning of life.' That's a declaration of love if I ever heard one, especially coming from a psychoanalyst! He is completely honest about it, admitting that his friends are more important to him than anything, calling it 'a need I have in me, something in the feminine part of me.' With Fliess, he shared a bisexual fantasy and argued so much on the subject that they broke off."

"He broke ties with all of his friends, in fact," Rebecca remarked. "Breuer didn't share his opinion on the importance of sexual factors, Brücke refused to accept his theories on the sexual origins of neuroses, Adler rejected the Oedipus Complex, Jung, in whom Freud saw his successor, had an affair with a patient, something Freud could not accept."

Amalia lost her temper:

"Does it make you happy to discuss my golden Sigi's latent homosexuality?"

Their line of questioning was much too aggressive for her liking. Why must they remind her that her son was inflexible and could not tolerate the slightest difference of opinion? Why did they insist on digging up his homosexual tendencies? Ferenczi had criticized him for being too rigid during a trip to Sicily in 1910, to which Freud replied: "Part of my homosexual investment in our relationship I removed and used to develop my own ego."

"Martha stayed with him until she died," Amalia added. "The only thing she ever reproached him for was for his practicing psychoanalysis, which she considered immoral. For someone as puritanical as Martha, it was worse than parading about naked."

"I can understand her point of view," Jeanne said.

Silent now, they gazed up at the sky. Had they reached a truce? None of them wished risking a falling out.

"I think that the end of a friendship is as painful as a romantic breakup," Jeanne observed.

"Oh no! You aren't going to start criticizing my son again, are you?" Amalia cried.

"I was thinking of Marcel, who disparaged all forms of friendship. He thought they were a waste of time that took him away from his novel. Nevertheless, he needed the company of others, a weakness he detested because, as he said, friendship 'is directed towards making us sacrifice the one real and . . . incommunicable part of ourself to a superficial self which finds—not like the other, any joy in itself, but rather a vague, sentimental attraction.'"

"It's true that his homosexuality complicates the matter," Amalia added. "None of his friends are above suspicion on that score."

"That's ridiculous! Everyone adored him. Some of his friends even visited him in the middle of the night. It was an honor for them."

And so the conversation went . . . Who would have the last word? They shot quotations from their respective sons as if they were poisoned arrows. Jeanne was the one who concluded at last:

"A true friend never judges and is always there for you. In fact, he's like a mother."

12

Cutting Ties

Very few people survive their mother.
Woody Allen

Yet, he loved her like a mother, and he hated her like a mother.
Albert Cohen

Coming into the world is not the same as being born.
Romain Gary

It was so dark in the living room that, at first, Rebecca hesitated. The blinds had been lowered and the curtains drawn as before a lengthy absence. She took a step in and discerned in the gloom the prostrate, immobile, seemingly overwhelmed figures of Amalia Freud and Jeanne Proust. Jeanne's hands were crossed on her lap. Amalia Freud was staring at the wall in front of her. They sat in silence, a glacial air lingering between them. What had happened? What would happen next? Rebecca observed them, torn between her curiosity and the fear that this microcosm of women where she had finally begun to feel at ease might be under threat. She felt like someone who has just learned she has a terminal illness: on the one hand, she wanted to know everything—the recommended course of action and treatment, its length and side-effects, chances of survival, statistics and whatever information she could get her hands on. On the other hand, she wanted to remain oblivious and still believe, hoping against hope, that the diagnosis was false.

Not knowing what to do to ease the anxious knot in her stomach, she wandered in the direction of what appeared to be a formal vestibule. There she found Pauline Einstein seated at a grand piano, playing the *Aria in C minor* from Bach's *Italian Concerto*. The energy and enthusiasm she put into her playing was out of keeping with the melancholy tone of the piece. Deeply moved, Rebecca stood listening a long while, until Pauline noticed her.

"I still can't manage to play it with the right tempo, after all this time," she said when she finished the last measure and stood up.

Rebecca begged her to continue.

"Would you like me to teach you how to play?" came Pauline's reply.

"Unfortunately, I have no talent for music."

"My son said the same about his skills as a cellist, yet he was a fine musician. Of course, I kept at him; I made him practice every day. I can't stop feeling that music is essential. For Albert, it was vital that he have a distraction from his work."

"Could you be persuaded to play something light and gay for the others? They're in a somber mood."

"I think you have something to do with that."

"What?"

"Your questions made them realize that their behavior with their sons was excessive."

"They only realized that now?" Rebecca burst out laughing with relief. Pauline, however, didn't share her comic view of the situation, and scolded her instead:

"What do you find so amusing? No one ridiculed you when you arrived here with a heap of insecurities of your own."

"You're right; it's terribly difficult to be a mother."

"I'm glad you agree. You have to indulge them a little. You've rattled these poor women."

"But the difference between us is that they never doubted themselves, whereas I always considered myself to be a horrible mother. With Nathan, I felt guilty about everything I did. I was bad-tempered, demanding and impatient. Like every single mother, I had too much to do and I criticized myself for not being available enough for him. I only had time to put out all the little fires that blazed around us: Why was there never any milk in the refrigerator on Sunday nights? Why did Nathan wait until after dinner when everything was closed to tell me he needed to photocopy a paper for school? Why did he lose his new winter coat in February, just when the stores were starting to carry summer clothes? How did his feet grow so quickly? I had to check on him in bed at least fourteen times every night if I ever hoped to get a minute of sleep. Whether I told him yes or no, I was sure he was going to wind up in the therapist's office. Just thinking about his future traumatized me. In fact, I'm rather happy I can finally rest here."

"You do seem different from when you first arrived: More self-confident."

"It's thanks to these mothers; I feel better just seeing their determination and their optimism. I realize now that they aren't as tough as I thought at first. I never imagined they could be hurt by anything I had to say."

Rebecca turned suddenly on her heels and rushed back to the living room. She wanted to open wide the curtains and the windows and talk to Jeanne Proust and Amalia Freud. She found them just as they had been before.

"I have to apologize," she began. "I'm sorry I riddled you with questions, but it was only to reassure myself. I was anguished over Nathan: he seemed to me too young to survive without his mother, as if age mattered. Thanks to you, I know now that I have already given him what he needs to succeed in life, whatever profession he chooses. Nathan is generous, happy, curious and considerate: I don't need to worry about him. My questions weren't meant to be indiscreet; I was only trying to understand your relationships with your children. I admired your sons so much when I was alive; it was exciting to go behind the scenes. I never intended to be critical of you or upset you; it was the furthest thing from my mind."

Amalia Freud stirred.

"I'm not angry with you, Rebecca, but you reminded us of things we'd rather forget. It's not your fault; you couldn't have known. Suddenly, I thought how ashamed I was on Sigi's seventieth birthday."

"What happened?"

"Well, my son had gone to great lengths to dissuade me from attending the party he was throwing at home. He was at the height of his fame and he had invited all his friends, colleagues, children and grand-children. I assumed he thought I would find it too tiring to come; I never thought he wanted to exclude me. I was so proud of his fame that I wouldn't hear of missing the occasion, and I was the first person to arrive. That's when I understood that he wasn't being polite when he told me not to come. When he finished his speech, I said to everyone, 'I'm his mother!' So pleased. In a fury, Sigi publicly repudiated me, and I still can't bear to think of it."

Amalia had gone ashen with the memory, which frightened Rebecca. She blamed herself and wanted to shake Amalia out of her mood, but how could she help such a strong-headed, intimidating, smart woman?

"Sigmund feared you as much as he admired you," she began. "Hatred and love are complicated emotions, especially for two people who were so close."

"You're right! Think of how he describes the mother figure in some of his texts: she's archaic, terrifying, castrating, sexual. She's a Gorgon who threatens to swallow him up, devour him, possess him. He must have derived his theories from me; what other explanation is there?"

"But he also says that a mother's love is 'the most perfect, the least ambivalent there is in all human relations,' and he idealizes the relationship between mothers and sons," Rebecca reminded her.

"My interpretation, unfortunately, is that Sigi's idealization of the mother was a way to compensate for his hatred of me. He opposed me in everything! I'm not stupid, you know. He even wrote this about me: 'As long as my mother is alive, she stands in the way of the rest I need.' As if I prevented him from doing anything! He couldn't wait for me to die; that's all there is to it."

"Maybe he didn't want to make you suffer by dying before you."

"I've heard that before and I don't believe a word of it. He was afraid of me, of my power over him and I was the Oedipal mother: seductive, dangerous, jealous, possessive . . . Did you know that

Sigmund had almost the same dream that Leonardo da Vinci had? He describes it in *Leonardo da Vinci and A Memory of His Childhood*. He dreamed that a beaked figure stole into his bedroom when he was a baby in his crib and that the bird 'opened his mouth with its tail.' He associated this with Egyptian hieroglyphs that depict the mother as a vulture. He's clearly describing his fear of a sexually menacing mother. Oh! I'm tired of all this."

Amalia collapsed back onto the couch and closed her eyes. Tears streamed down her cheeks.

"I was just rereading *The Problem of Anxiety*. I don't know what to make of this sentence. I'll read it to you: 'If writing—which consists in allowing a fluid to flow out from a tube upon a piece of white paper—has acquired the symbolic meaning of coitus, or if walking has become a symbolic substitute for stamping upon the body of Mother Earth, then both writing and walking will be abstained from, because it is as though forbidden sexual behavior were thereby being indulged in.'"

Rebecca was dumbfounded by the comparison of coitus and writing, walking and the mother.

"Freud was always writing, wasn't he? Countless notes, biographies, pieces of his autobiography, conference papers, lectures, prefaces, translations, essays, some twenty thousand letters. And he spent all his free time walking! He must have had quite an Oedipal complex!"

"So, why didn't he come to my funeral?"

"How do you know?" Rebecca asked, astonished.

"His biographers were very thorough, you know. They say that he sent my granddaughter Anna in his place, since he was too busy to pay me his last respects. Did I mean nothing to him?"

"No, of course not. He must have been afraid, not of you, but of himself: afraid to discover his own shame and guilt, terrified to realize how much he loved you and why he treated you so badly. Don't forget that he calls the death of a mother a 'crucial event.'"

"Maybe. Although he wrote that he considered his father's death the most important thing that ever happened to him. He always defended Jacob, but he would have been happy if I'd disappeared from his life."

Rebecca, who had by now integrated the customs of this unusual paradise, brought in a tray of hot chocolate with bread and jam and placed it on the coffee table. Amalia thanked her and began to serve herself hungrily. After she'd eaten everything on her plate, she was calm when she spoke again:

"It was my fault. As dictators, we were equals, but he went too far, and whereas he was respected as the patriarch of the family, I was dismissed as an ogress."

"Do you have an example?"

Amalia closed her eyes, thinking, then began to talk.

"Sigi was just horrible to Esti, his daughter-in-law, his son Martin's wife. He wouldn't let her choose her children's names, nor would he allow her to bring in her own pediatrician, whom she had loved as a child, for her own children. Sigi disapproved of him and there was nothing to be done to persuade him otherwise."

"She wasn't allowed to name her own children?"

Rebecca didn't dare imagine what her reaction might have been if her father had insisted on naming Nathan; she would have felt stripped of her role as a mother. But Amalia was fuming again:

"I didn't have any choice either when Sigismund was born, since Jacob's father had passed away a few months earlier and it seemed normal to name our son after him. It was later that he chose to call himself Sigmund. Nevertheless, Sigi insisted that his grandson be named Anton, after Anton von Freund, a Hungarian benefactor who had given a considerable sum of money for the construction of a psychoanalytic institute in Budapest . . . . Esti and Martin finally gave in. Sigmund's tyrannical ways went uncontested. His second grandchild, a girl, was named Miriam Sophie, Sophie being the name of his own daughter who had died in 1919 and the only name he would consider."

"Was he like that with all his children?"

"He was less dictatorial with his youngest son, little Ernst. The girls, of course, were treated differently: he insisted on supervising everything they did and he forbade them to work. Anna, his youngest, was the only one who stood up to him."

"How could you have been considered more formidable than him?"

"I was, nevertheless. My granddaughter, Judith Heller, said I was authoritarian, imperious and always in a foul mood. My grandson, Martin, said he would never forget my severity and my lack of empathy. He was referring to my supposed impassivity when my granddaughter, Mausi, committed suicide at twenty-three years old. She was beautiful, stunning, and she wanted to study medicine like her uncle Sigmund. In reality, she was depressed, something nobody saw, neither Sigi nor Anna, her cousin, though they were close. We couldn't have been more traumatized by her death. A year later, her brother drowned in the lake. He was nineteen. I was petrified by so many horrible events in such rapid succession, I didn't know what to do, or how to help Rosa, my daughter, who had just lost her two children. So I did nothing. I know she never forgave me. The worst criticism came from Dolfi, my youngest daughter, who lived with me until I died and blamed me for all her problems, including her spinsterhood. Everyone thought I was an insensitive monster but I kept my grieving to myself."

Jeanne approached the table, her eyes reddened by the tears she had struggled to blink back listening to Amalia. She poured herself a cup of hot chocolate, as if it might bolster her.

"Marcel dreamed of killing me, too," she stammered. "I never dared mention it."

She began pacing about the room, too agitated to keep still.

"How can that be?" Rebecca asked, startled. "After everything he said about you, everything he wrote about his extraordinary love for you!"

Jeanne Proust sighed:

"My little wolf came to the defense of a matricide case, he who could never do without me! Fortunately, I was already here when I read the article about this incredible story. I knew her well, Henri Van Blarenberghe's mother. She was a tall, tight-lipped, unattractive woman, who kept to herself. She was dedicated to her only son, but she never revealed anything, and talked only about superficial topics, such as fashion, the cost of living, or politics, seen from her limited perspective."

"Was she the murdered woman?"

"Indeed, may she rest in peace."

"Why did Marcel write an article about the murder?"

"Marcel was always so polite. When Henri's father died, he sent his friend his condolences, writing how distressed Adrien and I would have been for his loss had we still been alive. A few days later, Henri's response arrived, declaring his filial piety and describing how relieved he was to have his mother at his side in his time of mourning. Marcel relates all this in his article."

"There was no reason to suspect that Henri was in conflict with his mother or that he wanted to see her dead?"

"Nothing at all. Just as Marcel was preparing to write him back, he read in the newspaper that shortly after his father's funeral, Henri Van Blarenberghe killed his mother and then himself with a knife."

" Marcel must have been shocked that one of his friends could commit such a crime. So wasn't it normal that he would express his reactions in an article? He certainly didn't approve of the murder."

"That's true, but he never condemns the crime. What bothers me is that Marcel writes so coolly about such an atrocity, as if he had no relationship to the people involved. He quotes what were reported to be Mrs. Van Blarenberghe's last words, as her son was stabbing her to death: 'What have you done to me! What have you done to me!' Then he launches into an erudite analysis of the crime, comparing Henri first to Oedipus who pricks out his eyes with pins after learning of his mother's suicide, and then to King Lear embracing Cordelia's dead body."

"Marcel says that all sons are criminals. They 'kill all those who love us by the worries we give them.'"

Jeanne was too upset to listen anymore.

Rebecca brought in on a pretty platter of fresh pastries she had picked out to please Jeanne; having lived her life surrounded by lovely things, nothing saddened her more than sloppiness.

"If I were you, I would have been more upset by his short story, *A Young Girl's Confession*," Rebecca remarked.

"Why? It's the story of a young woman who is kissed by a common Casanova the day before her wedding. It's entirely made-up," Jeanne said.

Rebecca didn't want to disabuse her, but she felt sure the idea must have come from Proust's life. Even though the story is told from the girl's point of view, you'd have to be a dim-wit not to realize Marcel was the subject. The mother in that story also resembles the mothers in *Jean Santeuil* and *Remembrance of Things Past;* a loving worrier who is stingy with displays of affection. She nevertheless showers the girl with attention on her brief visits in order to "mitigate" her "excessive susceptibility." That sounded just like Jeanne: ambivalent and awkward, genuinely admiring at times yet more often critical. Marcel writes in *A Young Girl's Confession* that nothing bothered the girl's mother more than her "lack of will," exactly as it was for Jeanne with Marcel. He also has his protagonist say: "The realization of my fine projects for work, for calm and reflection preoccupied my mother and me above everything else, because we felt . . . that it would be nothing more than the image, projected into life, of that will created by myself within myself which my mother had conceived and nurtured." The relationship between Jeanne and Marcel is summed up in that sentence: their peculiar symbiosis and pathological identification with each other, their way of living vicariously through the other.

But Jeanne could not be swayed.

"You're talking nonsense! The mother falls from the balcony where she has been spying on the girl and her lover, and is killed. That seems quite unnecessary considering that the girl, who was twenty, knew what she was doing!"

Rebecca kept her thoughts to herself, namely how that scene seemed a precursor to the episode in *Remembrance of Things Past* where the narrator watches through a window while Mademoiselle Vinteuil and her girlfriend deface the portrait of Mademoiselle Vinteuil's father. What struck Rebecca more, however, was that, in the short story, the mother dies from the shock of seeing something she shouldn't have, "from my shining eyes to my blazing cheeks, proclaimed a sensual, stupid brutal joy." Proust has the girl say again: "I thought then of the horror of anyone who, having observed me a little while ago kissing my mother with such melancholy tenderness, should see me thus transformed into a beast." Wasn't Marcel writing about himself? Surely, if he had revealed his homosexuality to his mother, it would have killed her. And that, precisely, was the subject of *A Young Girl's Confession*.

To lighten the somber mood in the living room, Rebecca proposed they watch Woody Allen's short film, *Oedipus Wrecks*.

"It's incredibly funny: the protagonist admits to his therapist that he would do anything to get rid of his overbearing mother and even wishes her dead. His tone of voice is so offhand and casual, though, that you can't help laughing."

"I don't believe it," Jeanne declared.

"I'll just tell you how the movie begins," Rebecca said, hoping to convince them.

Sheldon, a dutiful son, takes his mother to a magic show. The magician invites her on stage, has her step into a box, and then makes her disappear. No one is more surprised than the magician, because nothing like this has ever happened in his act. Sheldon goes home alone, rejoicing; his mother has vanished and he had nothing to do with it. He hardly has time to get used to the idea, however, when his mother appears in the sky over Manhattan. Now she can watch his every move and scold him for acting like a little boy. She makes him feel guilty too: how could he be so ungrateful after everything she had sacrificed for him, her adored son?

"Wonderful! Let's all watch!" Amalia said, getting to her feet.

They gathered in a fully equipped multimedia room; there was a big screen, an impressive video library, all kinds of musical instruments and a stage worthy of a theater. Minnie, who frequently came here to watch and re-watch her sons' movies and television shows, was playing the harp when Rebecca, Amalia and Jeanne walked in without knocking, waking Mina, who had been napping in a row of seats, and disturbing Louise Cohen, who had been deep in a book by Philip Roth.

"We're going to watch *Oedipus Wrecks*," Rebecca announced. "Do you want to join us?"

Mina loved the movie; it reminded her of what Romain had said about her:

"I was trying to get rid of her, after all, of her overpowering love, of her overwhelming emotional pressure on me." She wasn't the least ashamed of her role as his overbearing, emotionally exhausting mother.

"You were his conscience, his *dybbuk*, his guardian angel," Rebecca observed.

"Exactly!" cried Mina, thrilled by the comparison.

Louise Cohen put her book down, the better to torture herself with the memory of Albert.

"Of all our sons, Albert was the most ungrateful. It's true he never tried to kill me, but he certainly mistreated me."

"Then, what do you make of *Book of My Mother*?" Rebecca asked, surprised. "It's thrilled generations of readers."

Rebecca couldn't understand how the most admirable of them all, the one who was the most loved, who inspired Albert Cohen to praise his mother's incomparable love, how could she have doubted her son's feelings for her?

"But don't you see that Albert's only talking about himself?" Louise replied. "The reason he wrote the *Book of My Mother* was not to glorify me, as you appear to think. No! He writes to absolve himself of his guilt. He knew he wasn't the best son and he also knew he should have come to visit me in Paris more often; he could have come any time by train from Geneva. He was too busy, though, poor boy, and it exhausted him to have to bear my adoring gaze as I begged him for a few moments of his attention. One evening, he lost his temper with me because I phoned up a countess who had invited him to dinner, to ask if my son, Albert, was still at her house. It was so late; I had started to worry. He could have had an accident. He was mortified by my intruding, with my foreign accent, and he let me know it! I was so humiliated. I begged his forgiveness, which made Albert think I felt guilty for what I had done. But I couldn't bring myself to face my shame. When did he become so selfish that he preferred the company of perfect strangers over that of his own mother?

Was that insensitive snob my Albert? I was so horrified that I burst out sobbing uncontrollably. I couldn't understand how things had gotten so bad between my little prince and me."

"How could you think that of his book? He worshipped you," Rebecca said. She had never gotten over his story of mythical filial love.

Unconvinced, Louise continued to provide her version of events:

"I think that the only thing that interested Albert was his writing. I was just material for his character, and a pathetic character at that: he describes me as having 'a rather large nose' and 'slightly swollen ankles' and he wrote that I was 'a bit ridiculous' as I 'lumbered along with one arm outstretched to steady my walk.' I can recite for you some other things he called me: 'a wicked fairy,' 'not very clever,' 'carefree,' 'awkward,' 'clumsy,' 'simple.' He even goes so far as to say I was a 'a poor, put-upon saint' who was 'born to be swindled' and 'a little unhinged by . . . distress.' But no matter how much I studied my reflection in the mirror to try to find that person he describes, I didn't see the least resemblance."

Jeanne couldn't resist bringing her own son into the conversation.

"Marcel thought that only people with a strong imagination were interesting; everybody else was mere material for his books. He also thought that the artist who interrupts his work to chat with a friend 'knows that he is sacrificing something that is real for something else which is not.' He couldn't have been more blunt. He didn't even spare me—his own mother! But I think I'm not the only one here to deserve such a treatment."

"You decry the fact that your sons altered you for the purposes of their stories, but that's the point: they weren't you. They're only characters!" Rebecca reminded them."

"You can't be serious! Even in their books, they wanted to kills us," Louise Cohen retorted. "In Albert's, he orphans Adrien Deume, and Solal refuses to see his parents because he's ashamed of them."

Louise had found more food for thought in *Portnoy's Complaint*:

"Do any of you remember how Alex Portnoy explains his friend Ronald Nimkin's suicide? I'll quote him: 'Because we can't take it anymore! Because you fucking Jewish mothers are just too fucking much to bear!'"

Jeanne was pounding noisily at the piano in a vain attempt to quiet her distress. The cacophony was intolerable. Mina came in looking for her and led her to a seat in front of the movie screen.

"Why don't we watch that Woody Allen movie?" Jeanne began before veering immediately back to the subject of her personal suffering. "We have every reason in the world to be devastated. Take me, for example: it pains me deeply that Marcel remains anonymous in *Remembrance of Things Past*. He's just 'The Narrator,' a character so formless that he doesn't even merit a description. It's obvious Marcel wanted nothing to do with me. That turns out to be complicated though: my little wolf has to twist his syntax to avoid naming him. Here's one example: 'He did not yet know me but having heard his comrades of longer standing supplement the word "Monsieur" when they addressed me, with my surname, he copied them.'"

"Albertine calls him Marcel," Rebecca reminded her.

"He also calls himself Marcel one time, but once in over three thousand pages doesn't prove anything."

Rebecca remembered how important names were to Proust. His infatuation with Albert Agostinelli, for example, led to his naming the Narrator's love, Albertine.

"Unfortunately, Marcel used his fiction to cover up what he didn't want anyone to know: that he was a Jew and homosexual. I never could bear that."

"You're not the only one who was hurt by the names our sons chose," Mina piped up. "Romain loved to use different ones."

"I thought that was your idea!" Rebecca exclaimed. "It's not true what he writes, in *Promise at Dawn*, that you told him he'd never become a French novelist with his Russian name? He says you even came up with some possible solutions: Alexandre Natal, Armand de la Torre, Terral, Vasco de la Fernaye... Pages and pages of names in fact. 'After each glittering parade of conquering names, we looked at each other, and shook our heads. No it won't do—it won't do at all.'"

"Maybe, but Roman Kacew was the one who came up with Romain Gary when he was completing his military service, without ever consulting me; I might have showed him how to go about it. He was also the one who decided to change his identity. It wasn't enough for him to be a pilot, a diplomat and a writer; he had to lead two or three different lives, and still he was never satisfied: 'The truth is that I was profoundly affected by the oldest protean temptation of man: that of multiplicity. ... I have always been someone else.'"

"Isn't that true for all writers, the desire to reinvent themselves and explore different lives?" Rebecca wondered. "You shouldn't take it personally. I'm sure they didn't mean anything by it."

"There are only two kinds of writers," Jeanne declared categorically. "The ones like Romain who believe in the myth of Proteus, and the ones who are much more like Narcissus, which was Marcel's case."

Rebecca wanted Jeanne to explain. She knew that Narcissus fell in love with his reflection and died of frustrated desire, but she couldn't remember who Proteus was. Jeanne scolded her as if she were a child who hadn't learned her lessons:

"Of course you do! Because Proteus could predict the future, Menelaus wanted to hang on to him but he changed into different shapes to escape: a lion, a snake, a panther, a boar, water, a tree . . . "

"Woody Allen made a film on the same subject. It's called *Zelig*."

"*Zelig?* What a ridiculous name."

"Well, it's a good movie. Why don't we watch it? You'll see!"

"What about *Oedipus Wrecks?*" Minnie demanded.

"We'll watch it after," Jeanne decided.

The movie began but no one could keep quiet. Jeanne kept up a stream of comments.

"To look at him, there's noting unusual about Leonard Zelig, but he's a regular Proteus: his skin turns dark when he's with people of color, his eyes turn up at the edges when he's with Asians, he claims he has a degree in psychology when he's with a psychologist . . . Such a chameleon, but no personality."

"Shh! Be quiet!" Minnie scolded her. "We can't hear anything!"

"This Mr. Zelig is the exact opposite of Marcel, who is the center of his own fictional world of Parisian high society," Jeanne continued.

"Like Albert, in his mythical Cephalonia," Louise agreed.

"Or Isaac Bashevis Singer in Krochmalna Street," Rebecca chimed in.

"Enough!" cried Minnie.

The lights came back on. Rebecca wanted to question Jeanne some more, but Minnie was ready to talk; she found her sons infinitely more interesting.

"The Marx Brothers were nothing like Proteus or Narcissus, although they did use nicknames. They only wanted to protect their privacy, not change their personalities or hide their real identities. All artists have stage names."

"Where did they get their nicknames?" Rebecca asked.

"Harpo took his name from his harp, Chico from his reputation with the 'chicks,' Gummo from his rubber orthopedic insoles, and Zeppo was invented by Chico randomly. Groucho is named after the 'grouch bag' he wore around his neck to keep whatever little money he earned safe… from Chico.

"That's how he got his name? I thought it came from his grouchy personality."

"That's true also, but not as flattering for him, especially after their given names were forgotten so completely. My sons became their personas, pure and simple. Harpo could never find a harp teacher who would teach him the correct way to play. They all said it was a waste of time with an autodidact like him. In reality, none of them wanted Harpo to play well; they liked him just as he was in the movies."

"And Groucho?"

"After inventing jokes for so long, he became the least funny of my sons: an uptight, moody intellectual."

"Just like Woody Allen," Rebecca remarked.

"You're not going to start begging us to find his mother again!" Jeanne exclaimed. "It's time for bed. We can continue this discussion first thing tomorrow."

Rebecca was amazed! Although time had no meaning for them anymore, they followed a schedule so strict it would have made a mother superior proud.

"Why do you want to sleep? Even when I was alive, I considered it a waste of time."

"Have more than enough time for anything now," Jeanne retorted.

"Rules were made to be broken," Mina chimed in. "Go to bed if you want, Jeanne. I'm staying up with Rebecca."

Louise Cohen got to her feet.

"As for me, I'm done talking for today."

"And I miss my pillow," Minnie said, stretching herself. "I always loved to sleep late and I never did it enough when I was alive."

Rebecca and Mina settled themselves on opposite ends of a couch with a warm plaid blanket between them. They were like girls at a sleep-over, thrilled by the prospect of a whole night of talk.

"Romain led many lives, and not just the ones in his novels. First Kacew, then Gary, then Emile Ajar. 'I was tired of being nothing but myself,' he said. But he had multiple identities already: Jewish, Catholic, French, Russian, Tartar."

"Didn't he publish *The Faces of Stephanie* under the pen name Shatan Bogat, pretending he was an unknown author and even inventing a biography for him? 'The son of a Turkish immigrant, Shatan Bogat is thirty-nine years old and a native of Oregon. He was formerly the director of a maritime transport and fishing company with operations in the Indian Ocean and the Persian Gulf. Arms trafficking was the inspiration for this novel. Bogat was awarded the Dakkan Prize in 1970 for his reporting on the international trade in gold and arms.' For good measure, he even wrote a different English-language version of the same book and said it was translated by one Françoise Lovat, whom he also invented."

"He finally did admit that he was Shatan Bogat, saying he had needed 'to take a break from himself for one book.'"

"Do you mind, Mina, if I read from *Treasures from the Dead Sea*, where Romain writes: 'Never before had I felt so intensely that I was no one, that is to say that I was someone.' He incarnated the characters that he created. He liked to confuse his readers, the better to stay in control of his identity."

"Yes, but it amused him as well. His system worked fine until he wrote *Gros-Câlin*, using the pen name Emile Ajar for the first time."

"I never understood why he hired his grand-nephew, Paul Pavlowitch, to pretend he was Ajar."

"That was madness," Mina said. "At first, he found it very amusing. He carefully instructed Paul on what to say in 'Shatan's' first interview with the press: that his real name was Hamil Raja, that he had gotten into some legal trouble in Brazil but was able to enter Switzerland thanks to a diplomat's daughter whom he knew, before writing *Gros-Câlin* under the pen name Emile Ajar. Paul finally let the cat out of the bag, and it went badly for them."

Rebecca was wondering why Romain Gary had committed suicide. Had he become trapped in his own lies, or lost his grip on his characters, or did he feel cheated of some glory that he deserved? Not long after the critics had destroyed Gary's book, *Your Ticket Is No Longer Valid*, which was the story of an aging, impotent writer, they acclaimed Ajar as a brilliant, modern new voice. Romain had never received that kind of praise when he published under his real name.

Mina was looking straight ahead, her gaze distant. After a moment, she shook herself and declared with conviction:

"Romain chose to die. It was his right. It wasn't like everyone says, that he was depressed or felt incapable of going on. He wanted to choose the moment when his life would end, not leave it to chance. He also couldn't bear the idea of getting old."

She smoothed her hair, slipped her shoes back on and stood up.

"In any case, he wasn't himself anymore towards the end."

Mina looked so sad that Rebecca had the impression that she could see right through her. Was she dreaming or was Mina becoming a ghost of herself, the kind of half-invisible phantom that people imagine? Were all these women going to gradually fade away right before her eyes?

To shake off this terrifying idea, and to bring Mina back to herself, she proposed with fake enjoyment that they go into the kitchen; they were sure to find whatever they would need to bake a cake.

Rebecca was picking at a plate of almonds, dates and an assortment of dried fruit while Mina, rolling pin in hand, formed a circle of dough, looking for a recipe for honey cake. Rebecca was trying to understand the reasons for Romain's suicide, and talking out loud was helping her.

"Romain's idea that 'loving is inventing,' that we are the creations of the people who love us, is an interesting one. Wasn't it you who said that what's missing in life is talent?"

"That's right. I must have taught him that, but, as usual, he put theory into practice and went too far," Mina replied softly. "That's how he created a legend of himself, inventing stories from nothing, even when they contradicted each other. For example, whenever anyone asked him where he had gone to school in Warsaw, he asserted he went to the French lycée, although he never was a student there because I couldn't afford the tuition. He would justify this piece of disinformation, saying, 'My mother did her best, why should I deprive her of the fruit of her labors?' He learned the art of fabrication from me. I loved the idea of my letters in *Promise At Dawn*; it touched so many readers."

"What? That's not true either?" Rebecca asked, shocked by this new falsehood.

"What of it? He makes me a heroine: the person I always dreamed I could be. He lies, but it's only to make me happy."

For Rebecca, however, this revelation changed everything; she had believed in the magnificent story of how Mina had taken the trouble to write two hundred and fifty letters to Romain, then asked a friend to send them to him one by one to make him believe she was still alive so he could continue to fight to liberate France from the Germans. But there was something else in this new deception that troubled Rebecca: if Romain imagined the letters, then he must have created them as symbols of his mother's oppressive, suffocating love, a love that was capable of following him from beyond the grave.

"How did he learn of your death, in that case?" Rebecca asked to hide her consternation from Mina.

"He received a telegram."

This time it was Rebecca who needed fresh air. Their long, uninter-rupted conversation had exhausted her.

She returned to the multimedia room to watch Woody Allen's *Decon-structing Harry*. She laughed at the protagonist, an egotistical author who draws the material for his successful novels from his relationships, but who finds himself struggling to write. Hounded by his characters who show up one after the other to lecture him, he is forced to concede that his own life is a disaster.

"Romain could have written that one," declared Mina, who had been looking for Rebecca. "Can we watch another one? I'm getting to like Woody Allen."

"How about *The Purple Rose of Cairo*?"

"Tell me the story first, Rebecca. I hate surprises. I always read the end of a book first: that way I'm never frightened, whatever happens."

"It takes place in New Jersey in the 1930s. Mia Farrow plays the heroine, who tries to forget the monotony of her married life and the troubles of the Great Depression by going to the movies. The dashing leading man in one of them jumps from the screen and appears before her, declaring his love. The other characters run off in fright while the producers, more annoyed than surprised, pursue their run-away star. The leading man discovers the world as it is, where cars don't await their drivers with the motors running and the lights on, where a fade-out doesn't prudishly hide what lovers do and where pregnant women have actual babies in their swollen stomachs, not pillows.

"I don't want to brag, but Woody wasn't the first person to think of that story. Romain wrote: 'Attacked by reality on every front, forced back on every side and constantly coming up against my own limitations, I developed the habit of seeking refuge in an imaginary world where, by proxy, through the medium of invented characters, I could find a life in which there were meaning, justice and compassion.'"

The film credits ran as the lights came back on, revealing Amalia Freud and Louise Cohen sitting in the back row. They burst into applause.

"That reminded me of Sigi's concept of the 'family romance,'" Amalia said.

"I can't say I see what you mean." Mina said.

"I mean that artists aren't the only ones with imaginations: perfectly ordinary people have some too. Sigmund exposed the fact that most children invent they have been adopted and suppose that their real parents are much younger, richer, more successful . . . In short, they believe that their 'real' parents make them more special than the people who actually raised them."

"Writers have more imagination than anyone. Not only did Romain eliminate his father from his 'family romance' when Arieh left me for a younger woman, but he created multiple fathers for himself, like Ivan Mosjoukine, whom I had told him so much about. But why don't we see him in person? He's the actor in the Russian film *The Queen of Spades*."

Mina jumped up to find the movie. It was filmed in 1916 and the reels looked every bit their age, but Mina saw none of the imperfections, only Ivan's beautiful eyes.

"He's certainly handsome, but what a boring film!" Rebecca said.

"Quiet, please!" Mina begged. "I can't hear anything."

"You're thinking he looks like Romain, I bet," Louise said.

"Obviously," Mina replied.

The lights came back up. Blinking, Louise Cohen had something to say.

"Albert invented an imaginary father, too. He liked to think that he was 'born by magic' and that his real father was a prince. He could never accept that a man as common as Marco could possibly be his father. He thought he belonged to a higher species entirely."

"Romain was just the same: he refused to believe his own genes. Do you know he once said that he had dermatological problems because of having 'inherited' someone else's skin?"

Amalia wanted to speak but the others wouldn't let her have a word in. Hadn't she been the one to start them on the subject and didn't that earn her the privilege of making herself heard? She thought she ought to demand that everyone be allowed an equal amount of time and that it should be strictly adhered to, like in presidential debates.

"As for Sigmund, when it came to choosing a father, he ignored the fairytales and the movies and went right to his half-brother, Philip."

"What!?"

"It's true. He actually wondered if Philip wasn't his father. You see, I was the same age as his half-brothers Philip and Emmanuel, while Monica, the aging governess whom we had hired, was Jacob's age. So it was natural for Sigi to think she was his wife, rather than me."

"If I understand correctly, he thought he was the son of his half-brother and the grandson of his father? It's no wonder he discovered the Oedipus Complex. You must have been a very attractive mother for him to marry you off in his head with this younger man. Did Philip deserve to be a father figure?"

"To tell the truth, he didn't spend much time with us."

"So you were completely available for your son," Rebecca said, warming to the idea of this 'family romance.'"

Mina seized the bull by the horns.

"Amalia, was Jacob Sigmund's father?"

Amalia blushed and stammered but said nothing.

"Because there are rumors, you know. Is there anything to them?" Mina continued. "Didn't you marry Jacob because you needed to get married as quickly as possible? In other words, you were pregnant! Why else would a happy, educated, pretty girl of barely twenty, like yourself, have married Jacob, an old man with no financial prospects whatsoever? Maybe Sigmund was right to think that the man who called himself his father wasn't biologically related to him."

"Absolutely not!" Amalia cried, horrified. "He called it a 'family romance' because it's all fabulation, a complete and utter invention. His doubts about who his real father was are just proof of the high esteem he had for me; it was a way of making me seem more desirable because the textile merchant I married was not good enough for me in his eyes."

"So he was in love with you after all!" Rebecca exclaimed.

"Whatever our sons reproached us for, they nevertheless set us on a pedestal, and sometimes idealized our characters of their novels," Jeanne said.

"It was the least they could," Mina agreed. "After everything we did for them!"

"Could we finally watch *Oedipus Wrecks*?" Amalia suggested.

13

We'll Live Forever

*For to one who loves, is not absence the most
effective, the most tenacious, the most inde
structible, the most faithful of presences?*
Marcel Proust, *A Young Girl's Confession*

*People are afraid of death because they can't
get it into their heads what it would be like
to live forever. Death is a kind of reward.*
Romain Gary

*Eternity is a very long time, especially
towards the end.*

Woody Allen

After having dissected their lives and those of their adored sons, after
having examined them from every angle, Rebecca's friends arrived at
a unanimous conclusion: they had done well! Sigmund Freud, Albert
Einstein, Marcel Proust, Romain Gary, Albert Cohen and the Marx
Brothers were all famous. They were the brilliant products of the education they had lavished on them. It called for a celebration. What better
way to crown the occasion than to throw a dinner party like they used
to give?

The decision was unanimous but there was much to be done and they
couldn't agree on everything. Jeanne was a perfectionist with the most
expensive tastes; there could be no dinner without flower centerpieces and
fine silver. For Minnie, the most important detail was the music. Louise

wanted to spoil herself for once with elaborate decorations. Amalia was happy with whatever they decided, as long as she would have enough time to make herself as beautiful as possible. Mina's primary preoccupation was the amount of food in the cupboards: would they have enough to eat? Rebecca was the only one who had no conditions: she loved all their suggestions.

The big evening arrived at last. The dining room glowed with candlelight and the flowers were exquisite. They took up their conversations where they had left them off, never so happy as when they were sharing marvelous stories about their sons.

Rebecca wore a long blue taffeta dress, and her hair and makeup were carefully done for the occasion. She was happy, beautiful, radiant. Her thoughts turned peacefully to Nathan. She felt at home among her friends, whom she was beginning to know so well, and their sons. They were so amusing, in fact, that she was finding it difficult to tear herself away from them to read a book alone or watch a movie.

The meal was festive. They feasted on delicacies of braised partridge and truffles and drank far too much champagne. Delighted by the immortality which their presence in this heaven proved, they were even more thrilled to be remembered on earth, where their names were still invoked. Yet the conversation turned again and again to their deaths and the moment they had always dreaded when they would finally leave their sons behind.

Jeanne was as dignified as ever in diamond pendant earrings and an elegant chignon.

"Marcel was so afraid of leaving me," she said. "All our lives we tried to accustom ourselves to living apart. But I knew he couldn't do anything without asking himself how I would have reacted. Marcel was thirty-four when I died, and I was sure he would not be able to bear the loss. However, he outlived me by seventeen years. I never imagined he would go on so long without me."

"But, since you knew him to be so dependent on you, when you were sick and the end was near, how did you prepare him for your death?" Rebecca asked. "It must have been terribly difficult for you."

"I never had the courage to tell him the truth. He was so fragile, so sensitive. To keep his spirits up, we played our old quotations game, as if nothing was wrong. By chance, I quoted Corneille to him: 'If thou art not a Roman, be at least worthy to be one; and if thou art equal to me, give better evidence that thou art.' It never occurred to me how cruel that must have sounded, that he would think I was exhorting him to be brave and to hide his grief."

"I'm sure Marcel didn't think you were quoting Corneille to be reproachful. Don't worry yourself about that. He knew you so well you didn't have to say anything to him; he could put himself in your shoes, just like the mother in *Sodom and Gomorrah* does with her own mother (the beloved grandmother of the Narrator), adopting her tastes and mannerisms the instant she dies. Marcel remarks how much they are alike: 'It is in this sense . . . that we may say that death is not in vain, that the dead continue to act upon us.'"

"Albert Cohen wrote: 'What is so terrible about the dead is that they are so alive,'" said Jeanne. "I think he's quite right."

Louise Cohen blushed with pride, as she always did whenever anyone quoted her son.

They were particularly animated in their discussion that evening, everyone speaking at once. Louise helped herself freely to the champagne and Minnie to the food, all the while struggling to keep her blonde wig in place.

"I was lucky. I couldn't have dreamed a better death," Minnie said. "The whole family was together, at Zeppo's house, on Long Island. There were seven of us at the dinner table, just like old times, and how we laughed and remembered: our shows in Texas, our illusions in Mississippi, our success on Broadway. And we finished off with a song! Afterwards, we played ping pong. I wasn't on top of my game at that point and my new wig kept slipping over my eyes. Chico won, I think. We laughed and laughed. The dinner was so good I wanted to start all over, so Zeppo, who always did as I asked, set the table again."

"You didn't really eat another meal?"

"It was a mistake no one should ever make. On the way back to New York, I began to shiver with cold. I remember I told my husband I shouldn't have eaten so much. Those were the last words I ever spoke. I began to suffocate. I felt like a fish out of water. Frenchie, my husband, reacted like a hero: he ordered the chauffeur to turn around, and, with a determination I never knew he had, jumped out of the car and stopped the traffic in both directions. We rushed back to Zeppo's; he was still doing the dishes. Frenchie carried me into the house and the doctor arrived but I heard him say there was no point in taking me to the hospital. My sons came to say goodbye, one by one, in order: Chico, Harpo, Groucho, Gummo and Zeppo. I knew I had to put on a happy face or they would become hysterical. It was the hardest thing I ever did: smile, though I knew I was dying. I waited until I saw each of them one last time before I let myself go. I don't know who was in the room when I felt a sharp pain: a brain hemorrhage. And then it was over. I had never heard of Woody Allen, but I have to agree with him that even if you're not afraid of death, it's better not to be there when it happens."

"Well, the main thing is that everything worked out for the best," said Louise. "We're here together in heaven, and the living still remember us down below."

"Because we were all mothers," Rebecca cried with delight.

Louise proposed a toast to motherhood and to mothers, in whom her Albert saw the archetype of all women, the Jewish race and its prophets.

"Sanctuary and consolation: that's what we are to our sons. Albert said it best: 'My mother's thoughts have fled to the land where time does not exist, and they await me there.' He knew I would keep for him all those stories of the Jewish ghetto in Corfu that he loved to listen to as a child."

Pauline Einstein arrived as they were getting up from the table. She was wearing a slim-fitting tweed blazer over a green skirt and she held a suitcase in her hand. She had the worried, hurried look of someone who has to arrive at the train station two hours early.

"Are you going somewhere?" Rebecca asked her.

"I am. I was made to be alone, just like Albert, who hated a crowd. This endless commotion's worn me out."

What had they done to drive Pauline Einstein away? It was true they hadn't spoken much lately of Albert, but why did she have to get angry about it? Unless she really did want to be alone like she said?

Minnie, who had a way with Pauline, had no intention of seeing her disappear again:

"What if we convinced Nettie to join us finally? She's always so amusing, isn't she?"

"Oh, that's a wonderful idea!" Pauline exclaimed. "I've missed her, and she loves to play mahjong."

"So, you'll stay?"

Pauline was back to her grumpy self as she stowed her suitcase in a closet and removed a folding card table, which she set up immediately.

"Will someone finally tell me what happened with Woody Allen's mother?" Rebecca demanded to know.

"I suppose I managed to exasperate her," Minnie said.

"That's true. You and your good mood all the time, always smiling and happy, and with such extraordinary energy and enthusiasm: nothing at all like Nettie, who spends her time complaining and cursing a life which seemed too difficult for her," Pauline agreed.

"How about the fact that you reminded her how much Woody Allen admired your sons?" Jeanne chimed in. "Rather insensitive on your part, don't you think?"

"Perhaps I did brag a bit," Minnie admitted. "But is it my fault if, in *Manhattan*, Woody Allen's character cites Groucho as the one thing that makes life worth living, before Sinatra and Brando, before Flaubert and Cézanne. Did I tell Woody Allen to say he was a Groucho Marxist? Did I write the screenplay of *Stardust Memories*, where a participant at a film festival claims to have written the complete filmography for Gummo, though he was never in a single movie? Is it so unbelievable that Woody Allen was a fan of the Marx Brothers? Why did Nettie have to take that the wrong way?"

"She'll be back eventually," Pauline said with the shadow of a smile. "She knows as well as I do that between our arguments and our apologies, we get along wonderfully. Just look at me: I'm staying, which just goes to show that it's impossible to leave you all."

"Have you heard this joke?" Rebecca asked, laughing already at the punch line. "What's the difference between French leave and a Jewish goodbye? In the first case, you leave without saying goodbye. In the second, you say goodbye but you never leave."

Minnie grabbed Pauline in her arms and spun her around the room, humming a tune. Rebecca began to sing "You Can't Always Get What You Want" at the top of her lungs, jumping and swaying in all directions.

"It feels so good to dance and sing and think about nothing! But have you even heard of the Rolling Stones?"

Pauline Einstein placed a mahjong set on the card table. Minnie rolled up the carpet, put on a foxtrot and danced with Rebecca. Amalia Freud, Jeanne Proust and Louise Cohen set up the mahjong, carefully counting out tiles. Mina took out a sheet of paper and wrote the names of the players to keep track of their scores. The dice were thrown and the game began.

Minnie and Rebecca went from tangos to the Charleston without missing a beat, laughing all the while. The only sound coming from the card table was the periodic announcement, in a serious tone, of a new set of tiles: pung, kong, mahjong.

Jeanne sighed noisily several times.

"If Jeanne is sighing, that can only mean one thing," Minnie observed, stopping the dance and catching her breath. "She's worrying about Marcel again."

Rebecca halted as well but kept time to the music with one foot.

"But we agreed! No more talking about the children!"

The End